VREHX

CONQUERED WORLD: BOOK ONE

ELIN WYN

VREHX

Streaks of plasma lit the blackness as a squadron of Valorni fighters swooped in dizzying spirals, blasting at the massive Xathi ship that filled the screens of the *Vengeance*.

We were so close it was the size of a planet. Like two steel ziggurats smashed and welded together. Not practical for space flight, but efficient enough to tear through several worlds.

Designed to intimidate.

Designed to destroy.

And we were going to stop it.

We crept closer, waiting. I sucked in my breath, geared for the inevitable.

I gritted my teeth as the bridge shook, and Karzin let out an undignified whoop from his station on the far curve of the bridge. The purple stripes on his shoulders rippled, and his excited eyes darted back and forth as if cheering on his favorite sport.

Barbarian. His crude Valorni traits got on my last nerve—not that he gave a rat's ass. Like the lot of them, he had no empathy for others. He barely listened to commands and forget anyone who didn't at least match his rank.

"You green motherfuckers aren't supposed to be hitting us, just laying cover for our approach," I snarled. "They can remember that much, can't they?"

They had only begun venturing into space when we took them into the alliance, but surely they weren't that stupid.

I hoped not.

"Fuck you," the Valorni drawled. The stretched-out sounds of his abominable accent were like bristles to my red Skotan scales. "Not their fault we're cloaked all to hell."

What an asshole. Valorni couldn't even be bothered to speak accurately. Their drawl made it nearly impossible to understand them, and they had idiotic slang for everything.

"They were informed of our flight path before the battle." The lights of Sk'lar's implants flickered in the dim light of the bridge. "It should have been simple for them to avoid it."

I smiled just a little, glad I wasn't the only one with some common sense. Sk'lar wasn't much better than Karzin, but he was more tolerable. My biggest problem was his implants.

His artificial augmentation was just creepy and wrong. You could see them light up in biohazard green against his shiny black skin. He looked like a fucking motherboard.

The strike team leaders were chosen for their specific talents and leadership, but Sk'lar's was not stealth outside the ship.

Karzin made it a point to butt heads with all of us. That usually distracted the rest of us from being at each other's throats.

Maybe that was his intention. Whatever. He was an asshole.

Karzin shrugged off the K'ver's barely concealed criticism. "Not gonna matter in a few minutes, is it?"

The sarcasm warranted him a disapproving side-eye from Sk'lar, which he ignored. I hated to admit it, but the jackass was right. In a few minutes, we would probably all be dead.

"Gentlemen," Rouhr's quiet word from the command station silenced the chatter, "are you prepared?"

The scar that ran down the left side of his face rippled as he clenched his jaw. He was annoyed.

Of course, we were prepared.

We shut up anyway. Rouhr was very diplomatic. That's why he was in charge.

We straightened ourselves and regained our concentration.

Tension and anger clogged the air, but there was no fear. Fear had died when our families did, when our worlds had burned under the Xathi attacks.

Around the half circle, each of us activated the new weapons panels, the long seconds drawing out as they lit up and hummed. Every battle had this moment—the waiting before the storm.

But this would be different.

We owned the storm.

"Let's blow a hole in those bastards," I growled, eyes fixed on the sickly green hull, thinking of the swarms inside.

They waited for the go ahead to surge through over the squadrons like locusts.

Nothing had been able to penetrate a Xathi hiveship before. They just plowed through and destroyed whatever they wanted, the swarms mopping up whatever the hiveship missed.

The Valorni, as annoying as they were, were inducted into the alliance for one reason. The Sugavians had worked with K'ver scientists using codialite, a mineral from the Valorni homeworld, to make one last attempt.

Just enough had been mined for this last-ditch effort —an experimental weapon that had a shot at penetrating that hull. It was rare, and we were on the losing end of this fight. We only had one shot.

We'd better make it count.

Every Skotan, K'ver, and Valorni warrior on the *Vengeance* had volunteered in the knowledge that it was a one-way trip. If this worked, the three strike teams below would board the Xathi and battle until there was nothing left.

If it didn't, we'd all die—just sooner.

Either way, the recorder satellites would beam the results of the experiment back to the scientists and engineers. We'd succeed, or they'd build a better weapon next time. That was the most important part of the mission, and we all understood how expendable we were.

The three of us locked focus on our stations as we crept closer.

"We are now in firing range, Captain," Sk'lar reported.

"Fire at will," was the only response.

Karzin sent the signal to the Valorni ships, and I started a slow count.

One.

His comrades had fought stupidly but bravely. There was no discernable pattern to the attack.

I was worried more would take friendly fire than would hit the Xathi, but they somehow made sense of the chaos, dodging fire from their comrades. If any survived the battle, they deserved to escape.

Two.

More likely the crazy bastards would follow us into the breach, but they'd earned the choice.

Three.

I activated the launch panel and braced, eyes fixed on the monitors. The adrenaline rushed through me in anticipation of the blow.

Nothing.

Not a bang or a pop or a whine. Just the hum of the engines, and the wall of the Xathi ship growing larger on the screens.

The anticipation deflated as I looked at the panel in confusion. The damn thing was experimental, but it should at least fire. The engineers weren't brain-dead.

With a snarl, I slapped it again.

And then the universe turned inside out.

JENEVA

I was in my element.

I was where I belonged.

Completely alone in the silence, except for the gigantic bipedal tree creature with an affinity for spewing poison.

Home sweet home.

A glob of the foul stuff hissed as it ate away the earth beneath me. It was only inches from my boot, but I didn't flinch or try to move out of the way.

A rapid movement around a sorvuc was far more dangerous than its projectile poison. Its damn branches were covered in tiny neural fibers, capable of detecting incredibly small movements. The fibers were illuminated purple.

The sorvuc searched for me.

Under different circumstances, I would have found it beautiful, but at that moment, it was just a pain in my ass.

The humidity made my short hair damp and scratchy. It clung to the curve of my neck. I longed to brush it away, but a movement like that would be a death sentence.

The luminescent purple faded away to a tranquil pink. I realized I was holding my breath.

Slowly, so slowly, I crept closer to the wide trunk of the sorvuc. I had already made an incision in its trunk. That's what pissed it off in the first place.

A necessary risk, but I only needed a few more drops of the thick scarlet fluid that seeped from the incision. The right person would pay a small fortune for its sap—or is it blood? Hell if I know.

As I slid my vial into place, ready to collect the liquid the sale of which would keep me comfortable for months, shouts erupted from somewhere nearby.

Damn it.

The sorvuc shrieked, its neural fibers flaring purple once again. It pivoted, razor-sharp leaves dangerously close to me. I rolled away, camouflaging my own movements in its rustling.

The hulking creature lumbered off in the direction the shouts came from—sort of. Its neural fibers must have picked up the sound vibrations, but with so many trees, it would have been difficult for the creature to determine the exact direction.

It's a good thing sorvuc had those fibers. They were as deaf as, well, a tree—at least, the sort of trees our ancestors brought over on their generation ship. But those trees sure as hell didn't fling poison or walk.

Walking plants were something the dense forest of Ankau had in excess. Even so, I'd take a hostile tree giant over people any day. At least they left me in peace.

Another round of shouts echoed through the trees. I clenched my teeth.

Speaking of peace.

I moved quickly and quietly through the dense forest, mindful not to disturb any of the thick vines that crisscrossed the forest floor. It was difficult to tell which ones were looking for a snack.

I spied a small herd of luurizi grazing between the roots of the docile Lenaus trees.

Their coats of lilac, sage, and pearl shimmered when they caught the mottled light bleeding through the canopy. Their silvery horns shone like jewels. It was easy to forget how deadly they were.

I was sure they could smell me.

Ordinarily, they would attack the moment they sensed an intruder. But this particular herd had become accustomed to my scent after so many years. It was an uneasy truce, but I still knew better than to take my eye off them.

Another bout of shouting brought me back to the present. It was louder this time. And stupider.

Clearly, whoever it was had a death wish, which was fine. I'd just prefer to be farther away when it happened.

The trees gave way to a small clearing. Two women, who I can only assume are the shouting morons, stood inches away from each other, their faces red with anger. They didn't notice my intrusion.

"You're not even trying anymore!" One woman, blonde and petite, hissed at the other. Her voice was tight, like she was trying to stay in control.

Sharp would have been the only way to describe her —sharp cheekbones, sharp chin, and sharp shoulders. Even her mouth was a sharp slash across her face.

I winced at her words, a headache throbbing at my temples. I almost wished something *would* come along and kill them.

"What more do you want me to do?" The other woman, dark-haired and softer than the other, answered wearily. "If I had known you were going to bring this up, I never would have agreed to meet you!"

Though they were different in coloring, they had the same nose and face shape. I guessed they were sisters—not that I cared.

"What other reason would there be to meet up?" the blonde snapped, her gray-green eyes narrowing. "What else do we have anymore?"

There was more poison in those words than there was in a fully grown sorvuc.

"I hate to interrupt," I said, startling both women.

I wanted to sound as annoyed as I felt, but my voice was brittle and raspy with disuse. I couldn't even remember the last time I had spoken aloud.

"But you really should shut up," I continued.

The blonde pivoted to face me. I was at least a head taller than her, but she somehow seemed bigger than she actually was. And the glare on her face would have made a narrisiri hesitate.

"This is none of your business," she said through clenched teeth.

"Nope, it isn't. I don't want to know about it. I don't care about it. But you really should find somewhere else to finish your screaming match," I replied.

"Do you think we're idiots? We have a howler with us," the blonde smugly fished a small black device from her pocket.

I hated those damn things. They emitted a high-pitched sound above the threshold of human hearing. It was meant to repel the creatures that stalked the forest, but I always thought it was a scam.

First of all, the people living in the cities and towns

hardly knew anything about the creatures that lived out here in the forest. Second, how would anyone know for a fact that a howler was working? No one could hear it.

"Yes, I do think you're idiots if you think that carrying a howler into the middle of aramirion territory during nesting season is a good idea," I snapped, fighting the urge to give the blonde a smug smile. "If they can hear that thing, you're screwed."

The dark-haired woman paled as she put her hand on the blonde's shoulder. The blonde stiffened at her touch.

"Leena, is that true?" the dark-haired woman whispered. Her eyes, the same color as the blonde's, nervously scanned the surrounding forest.

"How the hell would I know, Mariella? You're the one who moved all the way out to the middle of freaking nowhere!" the blonde, Leena, grumbled.

I turned to leave. Obviously, they had no intention of listening to me. Perhaps the dark-haired one, Mariella, might have seen reason, but Leena had some sort of chip on her shoulder—a chip the size of a damn ravine.

Fine. Whatever. They were adults.

I'd tried my best to warn them. It's not my fault if they chose not to listen to me.

What would I know, right? I've only been living out here for fifteen years. They would come to their senses and leave, or they would keep at it until one beast or another silenced them.

Either way, I got my forest and my silence back.

I could still feel their flurries of emotion as I marched through the undergrowth. If I was going to find another sorvuc to fill my vial, I needed to concentrate, but I couldn't do that with the feelings of two idiots in my head. I should turn back, try even harder to get them to leave.

A horrible screech unlike anything I had ever heard tore through the air. The sheer force of it drove me to my knees.

I tried to protect my ears with my hands, but it was useless. My vision blurred, stars danced behind my eyelids. I could practically feel my brain thrashing, desperate to escape that terrible sound.

Those idiots either did something to their howler, or the damn thing was malfunctioning. That had to be it.

As soon as I could get back on my feet, I staggered back to the clearing where I'd left the arguing pair. I would tear their stupid howler apart with my bare hands if I had to—anything to stop the noise.

"What the hell did you do?" I yelled.

Again, they didn't notice me when I entered the clearing, but, this time, they weren't distracted by an argument.

They stood side by side, looking up at the sky. Their faces were pale and their mouths were open in terror and confusion. I followed their gaze.

A jagged scar of pitch marred the once pristine stretch of endless blue.

The sky, *my* sky, had been torn open.

There was a beat of silence as if the whole planet had drawn in a collective breath of shock.

Then the forest erupted into chaos.

VREHX

Alarms blared around us. On the screen, all I could see were swirls of colors swallowing the Xathi.

The captain shouted orders to the rest of the crew, but his voice was distorted. It was changing—high-pitched then low and deep, fast then robotic, child-like then old, clear and loud, then soft and unintelligible.

Looking around the bridge, some of the colors were vibrant, glowing, and bright. Others were non-existent, as if all color had been drained, leaving behind various shades of gray.

Karzin's face twisted, melting down toward his midsection. I wanted to vomit, but Karzin's bird-like voice was chirping at me.

"TURN! IT! OFF!"

I turned my attention back to my control panel, just to see it swirl around and fade. The screen was so bright, my eyes burned. The letters seemed to be dancing an old Skotan wedding march.

Looking up at the screen, the Xathi ship was ripped apart by the swirling vortex—no, it wasn't a vortex.

It was just a hole. Then it was a rip.

The only thing that stayed the same were the colors. Purple, white, and red streaks of color were covering the Xathi ship and reaching out for us.

The part of the Xathi ship already inside the rip was separating, coming apart at the seams. I could see part of the Xathi crew floating in space, then shredded by the force of the rip.

And we were getting closer to it.

I heard Rouhr's voice yelling out commands, for the engine room to go full speed ahead and drive the Xathi ship further into the rip.

It made sense. If the rip was doing this kind of damage to the "top" half, then it should destroy the rest of it as well. If we went with it, so be it.

The engines kicked in, and we were rocked forward as we crashed the *Vengeance* into the Xathi ziggurat. Our momentum pushed the Xathi ship further into the rip, and I watched as more and more of their vessels were ripped and disintegrated. It was only a few short breaths before the *Vengeance* herself began to fall through.

The energy inside her was incredible. The air carried a charge that made my scales tighten and my hair stand on end. Every color I had ever seen exploded in my eyes, bringing me a level of pain I had never felt before.

My mouth opened to scream, but no sound came out. It was as if my throat was burning and ripping in half vertically. I felt my skin and scales peel away from my body, exposing my muscles and bones to the emptiness of the void.

My eyelids, clamped as tight as I could hold them, broke apart and fell away, slowly exposing my eyes to the grayness of the void we had entered.

The bridge of the *Vengeance* was a bright gray, and everything else was varying shades of gray, getting darker and darker.

I looked at Rouhr to see his body falling apart like sand. He was yelling at us, but there was no sound.

That's when I realized that there was no sound at all. There wasn't a single solitary noise. Was the rip in space this quiet or had my ears been destroyed?

I moved my hand to touch my ear and stared in wonder at the stump at the end of my arm. I looked down, and my fingers were on my lap.

I wanted to retch. I wanted to die. I wanted to close my damn eyes.

I looked up at the screen to see the ziggurat, at least the second half that we were attached to, reconstitute itself. It was rebuilding!

Then we were rebuilding, and the first of my senses to return was feeling. The pain was so much that I should have blacked out, except my eyelids weren't there.

When they finally returned, and I blinked for the first time, tears fell down my face. Finally, sound came back with an explosion of noise.

"...the hell is happening?"

"...are we?"

"Damage reports!"

"...off the damn switch."

"...switch, Vrehx!"

It felt as though forever was passing before my mind caught on to what they were wanting. I looked at my control panel and flipped the switch to the weapon. The void ended, and the alarms were back.

"Where the hell are we?" Rouhr asked.

"I'm not sure, Captain!" Sk'lar answered.

"Scan the—" Rouhr was interrupted as the ship shook violently, knocking most of us from our seats. "By all that is holy, what was that?"

Engineer Thribb's voice came on over the intercom.

"We're losing engines, Captain. Partial power only. We've been caught by a gravitational field of some sort."

"What is generating the field?"

"I'm not sure, sir. My systems are inoperative."

"Sk'lar!"

"On it!" Sk'lar checked his system, letting out a curse that the translator didn't bother to translate. There was no need. "We're above a planet. Unfortunately, we are falling toward it."

He tried to keep his voice calm, but the slight vibrato betrayed his emotions.

The *Vengeance* wasn't built for the atmosphere of a planet. Our thrusters wouldn't work. If we fell into the atmosphere of a planet, we'd fall until we impacted with the ground, and it would be a very hard landing.

"Sir! The Xathi!" I called out, pointing at the screen.

The Xathi ziggurat was tilting, as if it were falling as well. Outside scanners adjusted and brought the full picture into view.

The planet was covered in green and blue, and above it, the Xathi ship tilted ever more as it fell.

"What planet is this, and where are the Xathi going to land?" Rouhr asked.

I brought up our positioning and the star maps in our database. "Sir, this is uncharted space for us. We don't have this planet or this system in our database."

Rouhr nodded, absorbing the information. "Crash site?"

Sk'lar turned to look at me, then at Rouhr. The look on his face was silent resignation that something bad was going to happen.

"There appear to be seven main points of population on the planet. The Xathi are going to crash into the biggest concentration," Sk'lar said.

"Estimated survival?"

"Not good. Easily half of their city will be destroyed, killing thousands."

"And what of the Xathi? Will they survive the crash?"

"I'm not sure, sir. I'm not sure what the interior makeup of their vessel is, so I couldn't give you an accurate guess," Sk'lar replied, refusing to look at Rouhr as he stared at the computer.

"Engineer Thribb?"

"Captain?"

"Any chance of us breaking free and *not* crashing on the planet below?"

"Less than three percent, sir."

"Well, *groop*." We all looked at Rouhr in shock. "Any way to get us away from civilization?"

"Easily, as long as our engines don't finish cutting out on the way down."

"Then keep us away from any population centers.

The rest of you, brace for impact!"

We watched the Xathi ziggurat crash into the center city, the largest city, as we strapped ourselves into our seats.

The cloud of dust and flame took out half of our sensors as we entered the atmosphere. We gained speed and tilted forward, and I could feel the pressure of the straps trying to hold me up as gravity pulled me downward.

It was a struggle to breathe. The pull of gravity was forcing us downward, while the atmosphere tried to resist our penetration. I tried to lift my arm to my console to push the button for the retro rockets in order to level us out and slow us down, but I couldn't lift my arm high enough.

The ground rushed at us, and I closed my eyes.

I'll be back with you soon, my family, I thought. My only hope was that we took those bastards with us.

My head snapped forward as the *Vengeance* crashed into the ground.

There was no way that death could possibly hurt this much.

I looked to my left to see Karzin slowly and gingerly lifting his head. Just past him, S'toz's head hung forward, his chin on his chest. To my right, Sk'lar was moaning in pain, trying to reach his arm up to his head.

I slowly—oh, so, so slowly reached up to unbuckle

my straps. Now free from my restraints—and oh so grateful for them, as well—I gingerly got to my feet, waiting for the blast of pain to overwhelm my senses.

"Location?" I asked.

Sk'lar answered after a short coughing fit. "We're planet-side. That's all I know. Last thing I remember seeing was that we were heading for a large forest."

That's when it finally hit me. The computers were down.

"Captain?"

A groan from behind Sk'lar answered us. Rouhr's straps had snapped, and he ended up being flung around.

"I'm still alive. Vrehx?" He pulled himself to a sitting position on the floor, his right arm dangling, blood flowing from his cheek, and his left arm clutching his ribs.

"Sir?" My left arm hurt, and it was hard to breathe, I might have cracked a rib or six. I had a headache from the depths of destruction, and I was struggling to maintain weight on my right ankle.

"Get the commanders and your teams together. Find out where we are and if we're in danger. Thribb and I will handle the ship."

I knew better than to argue with him.

I made my way to the lift, but the doors wouldn't open.

I moved three steps to my left and opened the maintenance hatch. Looking down, it was surprisingly clear.

Time to climb, I thought.

At least it was downward.

JENEVA

When the large thorn of the approaching Zanium plant ripped the back of my shirt, I knew we were in trouble. Not just any trouble, but a shitload of trouble.

My eyes darted around, desperate to assess the situation. The clearing wasn't a remotely safe place anymore. It seemed as if the lethal flora and fauna around us had gone mad.

Maybe it had.

Maybe whatever had ripped open my sky had cursed us.

The two women were at least quiet for now. I'm not sure if I should have been pleased they hadn't fallen prey to the range of creatures lashing about—yet. I supposed there was some comfort in numbers, though it would have been easier to only look after myself.

The broad-leaved, spiky-thorned vine Zanium was not our only problem. It was just a significant part of the current trouble.

Zanium travels rapidly across the ground, zigzagging along, in the camouflage of other vines. Any other time, I'd have no trouble getting away from it.

Now was not like any other time.

A shiver ran down my spine as my mind worked overtime. Thoughts tumbled over each other. Escape plans formed before being discarded again.

"Eiiii!" I heard one of the women screech.

I glanced at her, shooting her icy stares. Why the fuck was she screeching like an injured grizsk?

There was no blood oozing from any of her body parts. Her limbs were still attached, as was her head.

The words of rebuke died on the tip of my tongue when I spotted the source for the mad scream.

Not a griszk.

Something worse.

To our right, I saw black saucer-eyes with a tinge of red in them fixing on us. Despite the body still hidden in the rapidly thickening bushes, I didn't need to guess what creature the eyes belonged to.

Aramirion.

Ice fingers raked through my insides. They hovered

over my heart, slowly wrapping themselves around it. Breathing became difficult.

Get a grip! I chastised myself.

Turning into a fumbling idiot was not going to help. Quite the opposite.

It seemed that the creature was too far away to use its poison.

Whilst aramirions were known for their accuracy, they lack distance. At their best, they can shoot fifteen feet.

This one, if indeed there was only one, was three times that distance from us. It meant we had some time. Not a lot—maybe about fifteen seconds before it would leap closer to kill us.

"Do something," whimpered one of the women behind me.

I couldn't work out which one. Didn't really matter. If she wanted something done, why didn't she do anything?

She clawed at my arm, her fingers digging into my flesh.

I resisted the temptation to punch her. If I knocked her out, I'd have to carry her—a burden I didn't need right now.

"Just shut up," I hissed at her without taking my eyes off the enemy.

Never let yourself be distracted. It's the ultimate

mantra, the one you never break. Breaking it could spell your death.

"Look behind us," I commanded my semi-hysterical unwanted companions. "Tell me what you see."

With my eyes fixed on the lethal killing machine, I waited for the description.

Nothing.

There were plenty of sounds, just not what I wanted to hear. The world around us teemed with the angry war cries of the creatures inhabiting this part of the forest.

"What can you see?" This time I don't hide my anger from my voice.

"I...green...puuuurrpp..." one of them babbled. None of what she stammered made any sense to me.

Crap, what was I going to do with this lack of info? Back up and away from the mutant green, eight-legged monster spider? What if I backed us into another, just as deadly, foe?

"I need to pee," I heard one of them whisper.

"You'll have to hang on," I snapped. "I need to know if we can go backwards. I don't want to take my eyes off the aramirion."

I heard a wail and shook my head. Could this day get any worse?

Mentally, I prepared for a quick backwards glance.

If I got one second, I'd get a glimpse at least. It needed to be done.

Nothing too bad behind us. At least, not that I could see in the second I had to assess the situation.

With outstretched arms, I started to move away from the green killing machine—except it had taken advantage of my breaking eye contact with it and moved.

Now, I had no idea where it was. The green of the vines, bushes, and trees provided ample opportunity for it to hide.

The thud on the ground made my head snap around. One of those massive tree trunks had taken a step toward us.

At the same time, the aramirion reappeared.

And now it was on the attack.

Green flashed past, I pushed the women backward and onto the ground before I curled into a ball to roll out of the way.

I hadn't been fast enough. One of its legs scraped across my shoulder, leaving a large gash. My skin burnt and blood trickled out of the wound.

My eyes searched the ground. The mutant spider had already spun around for another attack.

"Grab something! Anything!" I shouted at the two women.

By now, my knife was in my right hand, and a large

tree branch was in my left. I swung the long piece of wood above my head.

Killing the creature was hard. The exoskeleton was too tough for a blaster, let alone my knife or stunner.

All I could hope for was to wound the creature to the point where it would leave us alone long enough for us to make a run for it.

If I could get close enough without getting killed, I could attack those legs.

I watched, wide-eyed, as it took two bounds to be on top of us. The acid spewed forth as it came at us, missing me by the smallest of margins. I wasn't sure about the others, but I hoped they'd rolled out of the way, too.

As the creature hovered above me, getting ready to pick me up, I stabbed its legs as hard as I could.

Green liquid started to ooze from the wounds I inflicted. Now it howled in anger and pain. It stumbled away from us, not before ripping into one of the women.

"Noooo!" the other screamed.

I felt one of them tug at my arm, the one with my injured shoulder. I winced in pain.

"She's hurt, help her! Mariella's hurt!"

I ignored her. There was nothing I could do—at least not until I'd dealt with the angry spider. It would kill us.

As I waited for the creature to regain its balance, I felt the breeze in the back of my neck get stronger. Sometimes, it takes just a few minutes for the gentle breeze to turn into a fierce storm.

A storm was the last thing we needed.

I crouched down as the injured aramirion righted itself from a stumble. Half turned toward us, it lunged.

My knife was at the ready. This time, I was going to go for the eyes.

It was four arm's lengths away.

Three.

Out of the corner of my eye, I detected movement. A large green branch—no, a trunk, had started to move. What was coming to the aid of the mutant spider, I wondered?

Before I knew exactly what had happened, the tree, one of the few ordinary non-killing trees we had here, crashed onto the creature. It landed fair in the middle, squashing the spider flat onto the ground.

Mesmerized, I watched the legs spasm a few more times, as if wanting to move forward, before the creature lay there, dead.

"Please," begged the woman whose name I'd already forgotten. It snapped me out of my trance.

I looked around. Her friend was lying on the ground, bleeding.

"Help her to her feet," I told her friend and moved to

one side. I ran over options while we picked her up and hurried out of the clearing. There was no way we'd make the village.

Not far was a cave. I'd sheltered there before during storms.

"You need to help her."

I fixed the hysterical woman with an icy stare.

"I can't do anything here. Those things hunt in packs, and it won't be long before its two mates find it. And us."

VREHX

Green.

Nothing but intense, eye-searing green.

My right hand reached into the belt around my waist to pull out eye shields. Instantly, the throbbing in my head eased. Now I didn't have to squint to glance around.

We headed into what looked like the least densely covered area of the jungle, moving as swiftly and silently as five large warriors could manage.

My own movement was abruptly stopped when, midstride, I couldn't shift my leg anymore.

"What the fuck?" I muttered.

The other two, who'd been flanking me left and right, kept moving past me.

"Not time for a break yet," grunted Tu'ver without looking at me.

It took several seconds for me to realize a fucking vine had wrapped around my boot. When it didn't come off with a simple sharp pull of my leg, my right hand grabbed a short knife from my belt.

One quick slice through the fibrous stem and I should be free—or so I thought. What I hadn't counted on was the fact the vine was faster than me.

Before I'd even managed to cut through the entire thing, more leaves covered my boots. Their hold tightened.

"Stop srelling about and keep moving!" shouted Axtin, a few strides ahead of me by now.

Instead of hurling an insult at the man, I took out my blaster. After I shot several rounds into the ground around my foot, the rest of the plant shriveled up, and my leg was free.

"What the srell..." Axtin spun around to glare at me.

Further words died on his lips as the ground shook beneath us, and we all heard the same thud, thud, thud.

Whatever was approaching was monstrous.

"This way," Tu'ver waved us to where he stood.

I took a moment to glance around.

Before any of us could take another step, we were surrounded by thin, delicate, deer-like creatures. They looked elegant, even pretty. The animals' bodies had a light brown fur covered in tiny white dots, as if paint had accidentally been splashed on them.

"Don't make any sudden moves," I urged my teammates as I tried to move toward them without drawing attention to myself.

"Why not just shoot the fuckers?" growled Axtin, already holding one of his many weapons in his left hand.

"Because we don't know if they're peace--" the rest of my words died in my throat as the four-legged creatures with the enormous dark brown eyes leapt toward us.

I spotted the shimmering silver spikes protruding from the animals' hooves.

"Can I shoot now?" Sarcasm dripped like poison from Axtin's voice.

My blaster was my response.

If I'd thought this was going to be a stroll in the desert, I'd thought very wrong. Shouldn't have assumed these creatures weren't killers simply because of their incredible beauty.

Two leaped for my head. At the last second, I managed to roll out of their way, aiming at their bellies as I did so.

One was hit. It plummeted to the ground. Blood and guts spilled out of its ripped open belly.

Back on my feet, I looked around. My eye shields

had fallen, now covered in what was left of one of the creatures.

The rest of my team had killed their attackers. The herd retreated, obviously not wanting to suffer the same fate as those on the ground.

Axtin dodged around a knobby-looking tree, but it flicked its tendrils at us.

Tu'ver was about to use his arm-length machete to slice through the moving branch when the cream bud on it opened up to release three-eyed winged reptiles, each the size of our hands, spitting garish violet fluids as they swooped towards us.

"Damn!" shouted Axtin. "It's some sort of acid!"

His suit sizzled, repairing itself.

Tu'ver didn't need a written invitation to use his guns. With cold precision, he knocked each out of the sky until the air was clear again.

We came to a trickle of water, not even a creek. I stopped my men before we crossed. It was hot.

Axtin crouched down. "Could be acidic." He turned toward Tu'ver. "Might short circuit your electronics."

"You look after yourself," grumbled Tu'ver, crossing the obstacle with one large stride.

The impossibility of our warring species remaining united to defeat the Xathi weighed on me, and not for the first time.

Once I, too, crossed the blue water, I hesitated. I was

half tempted to take a sample back to our ship.

We'd been sent to investigate. Would it help to bring back a sample? What if we ran out of water?

Before I could act, there was a rustle in the low green and purple bush growing right at the edge of the water. I spun around just in time. Without waiting to see how this animal was going to try to kill us, I activated my blaster.

After I'd shot the creature, I took a quick glance at the scaly body, giving its last writhe on the ground. The animal had the body of a massive snake with yellow spines along the back and a red stinger on the tail.

Lovely.

Finally, we came to a small clearing.

I sensed it was not safe to linger at this over-exposed area. At least in the forest of lethal plants, there were places to hide and use in fending off violent attackers.

"Which way?" Tu'ver looked at me.

Axtin was about to respond when I held up my hand.

A strange howling could be heard. It was hard to know exactly where it came from.

"Let's head this way," I told the others before I made for a well-trodden path.

"But—"

"Now," I commanded.

"We've—"

"Now," I repeated before I stormed off.

"What the srell?" Axtin's voice behind me roused me out of my own thoughts.

Instinctively, my hand reached for my weapon as my eyes searched for the next monster about to attack us. It took a minute or two for me to see what Axtin had noticed.

Could have been shock or something else, but when I saw three women at the mouth of the cave, I lowered my own gun. The rest of the party did the same.

When the tall one fired a shot, dirt, leaves and grass ripped up in front of me. Some of the debris hit me in the face.

Axtin reacted first by reaching for his blaster. He stopped mid-reach when the round of fire ripped up the ground in front of him.

"The impacts are not consistent with a heavy blaster," Axtin reported, "but most likely an energy field set to a low stun."

Another shot threw up some dirt.

"Still srelling dangerous," Tu'ver muttered.

He was right. Looked like these women were as vicious as the rest of the flora and fauna we'd come across. Or maybe just frightened.

Question was, what the fuck were we going to do about it?

JENEVA

I considered myself a relatively easy-going person. I'd survived living in a jungle, on my own, for years. I couldn't have done that if I kept losing my temper.

It was already bad enough that the sky was breaking apart above us. I was shaken up after our narrow escape from the aramirion. Mariella was losing blood so fast, I didn't know if there was anything I could do to save her.

The last thing I needed at that moment was to be backed into a corner by a group of monsters.

And not even my normal monsters.

Firing that stun gun felt good. Damn good.

"Back off! Next time I won't miss!" I snarled. They didn't have to know my weapon was merely a stun gun.

In the murk of the cave I had initially mistaken

them for humans, but I was very wrong. They were
humanoid in shape, but far more muscular than even
the most seasoned laborer in the colony. And no man
I'd ever seen came in those colors.

Oh.

The sky ripped open. It would be stupid of me to
think that the sky simply did that on its own.
Something made it happen.

And now, three strange non-human creatures with
battle gear and heavy weapons were standing before
me. The sky ripped open, and something came through.

Aliens.

Years of dealing with unfamiliar creatures in the
forest prevented me from going into a complete panic. I
took a steadying breath and observed them.

The one on the left appeared to have intricate green
circuits melded with his gray skin. Or perhaps it was a
skinsuit. It was difficult to tell, though I really didn't
care either way.

He was bald and, although shorter than the others,
still taller than me. His black eyes were endless and
unsettling. I quickly looked away.

On the right stood a juggernaut of pure muscle, the
largest and tallest of them by a longshot. He looked
strong enough to tackle a sorvuc and not die. Well, at
least not immediately.

His green skin had deep purple bands wrapping

over his shoulders and around his arms, his equally green hair nearly reached his shoulders. His eyes were dark, not pitch black like the smaller one, but an earthy brown. Still, there was no warmth in them.

With the amount of weaponry he was packing, I figured he would be the one to watch out for.

I didn't like the idea of taking my eyes off him. He could be like the Zanium vines that snake across the forest floor. It's when you stop watching them that they become dangerous.

Almost against my will, my gaze settled on the third alien at the center. Immediately, I noticed the intricate pattern of scales over his skin, both the burning red color of a dying sun.

His eyes were red, too. They looked like embers in the inky light of the cave.

Compared to his skin and eyes, his close-cropped black hair was a startling contrast. His scales appeared to be shifting slightly of their own volition.

Under different circumstances, I might have found those scales fascinating. I wondered what one of those scales would fetch on the market.

There were two more creatures—aliens—stationed at the mouth of the cave. Their backs were to me but I could see another red-scaled one and another green-skinned one. They didn't seem to have any interest in us.

The trio standing before me exchanged a look. The gray one grunted something. The green one responded in kind.

The red-scaled one turned back to face me. He stepped forward, reaching for something on his hip.

"Don't. Take. Another. Step." I hissed, holding the stun gun so it was level with his chest. It was a broad target that would be hard to miss.

Whether the red-scaled alien could understand me or not, he clearly got my meaning. He stopped, retracting his hand from his hip and lifted his hands in a gesture of surrender. I didn't lower my stun gun.

He had the nerve to give an exasperated sigh as he reached for something else attached to his bandolier. He unsheathed a small knife made from a dark, almost black, metal.

I blinked in confusion as he extended one scaled arm.

The scales rippled and retracted, leaving behind a smooth skin of the same color. His scales were essentially built-in body armor. Fascinating.

My mind exploded with questions. Were the scales formed from hardened skin, plating, or bone? If one fell off, would another grow back?

I made myself stop. Maybe later I could get one, check it out.

He lifted the dark knife to his exposed skin, wincing

as he quickly drew the blade across it. Cobalt-blue blood dripped onto the cave floor. The other two shouted in alarm, something that translated clear across the language barrier.

"What did you just do?" I demanded.

I had encountered enough strange creatures to know that blood could easily be weaponized. At least on this planet, it could evolve to a corrosive poison or an airborne toxin.

The red-scaled alien didn't deign to answer me or even acknowledge that I'd spoken—not that I would have understood him anyway. With his good arm, he fumbled again for the parcel at his hip.

After a few moments of struggling, the gray-skinned one stepped forward and grabbed the pouch. He opened it, pulling out a small device. I couldn't even begin to guess its purpose.

As the gray-skinned one moved, I noticed that the circuits adorning his arms and shoulders flickered and glowed faintly. He handed the little device to the red-scaled one, who held it up to the gash in his arm. It pulsed with energy as a pinpoint of white light passed over the wound, flickering where it encountered torn skin.

I watched in awe as the strange light stitched the red-scaled alien's skin back together. When it finished, there was barely a scar.

He extended the hand, holding the device toward me, and looked at Mariella. I nodded in understanding and lowered my stun gun.

"You're insane if you think you're using that thing on my sister," Leena snapped.

Mariella's head was in her lap. She was far too pale and could barely keep her eyes open.

"She's going to die if we don't do something," I said, trying to keep my voice gentle. Even if I thought Leena was annoying, it must be horrible for her to see Mariella like that. A thought of my own sister flashed across my mind, and I pushed it away, where it was safer.

"It won't work on us," Leena said, as if it were the most obvious thing in the world. "Didn't you see his blood? It was blue. It doesn't react with oxygen the way ours does, which means his blood has a completely different composition. That device likely won't even recognize her blood."

The red-scaled alien said something in his incomprehensible language. He was looking at Leena. His eyes narrowed.

If I didn't know any better, I would say he sounded annoyed. At least I wasn't the only one who found Leena irritating.

"Do you have a better idea?" I asked.

"Not using the unfamiliar alien tech is the better

idea," Leena shot back.

"Look," I said with a sigh, "if we don't do something, Mariella isn't going to make it. Wouldn't you want to do everything possible to give her a chance of survival? If she dies, how are you going to live with yourself, knowing you didn't explore every possibility?"

I know I sounded harsh, but I didn't have time to deal with Leena's stubbornness. Mariella certainly didn't either.

Leena looked down at her rapidly fading sister and ran her slender hands through her sister's dark hair.

Mariella's pale eyelids flickered. Sweat beaded on her forehead.

"Okay," Leena said softly. "Do it."

"Maybe we should let the alien do it," I suggested, suddenly nervous.

"No!" Leena said firmly, fixing me with a steely gaze, her intensity almost a physical rejection. She turned her glare on the aliens. "I don't want them anywhere near her."

I knelt down beside Mariella and examined the device in my hands. There wasn't much to it really. Oblong in shape, black and shiny, with a divot on one end where that white light must have come from.

I mimicked the way I had seen the alien hold it. I looked back at Red. He was watching us with a stoic expression.

"Like this?" I asked, indicating the way I held the unfamiliar device.

He nodded once.

I moved the device a little closer to Mariella's wound and it hummed to life. I moved my hand up, allowing the flickering light to pass over the worst of the wound. I hadn't realized I was holding my breath until I gasped in relief when Mariella's wound began to close.

"It's working," Leena sighed. Her voice was tight as if she was on the brink of tears.

I directed the light over the wound twice more before it was fully sealed. I didn't have the skill of the alien; Mariella's skin was marred with a pale scar, but she would live.

Color slowly returned to her face. Her eyes fluttered open. "Leena?" she asked, her voice hardly more than a croak.

"I'm here, Mari. You're going to be fine," Leena soothed, petting her sister's hair.

I stood, letting the sisters have their moment. I warily approached the red-scaled alien, stopping just far away enough to give him back the device.

"Thank you," I said.

He simply nodded.

Now what?

VREHX

We couldn't stay here much longer.

It was only a matter of time before the wildlife found us in here. For all I knew, one of those sentient plant monstrosities was already inside with us.

Hell, I wouldn't be surprised if the rocks came to life and started attacking us.

And we still didn't know where the Xathi were.

The three creatures huddled before us were certainly willing to fight back. At least one of them was.

They were clearly of an intelligent species with a language and a cognitive understanding of their environment. They must be the local dominant species. Whatever information they could provide would be useful to our mission.

"Tu'ver, radio in and let the *Vengeance* know we'll be bringing the intelligent lifeforms on board," I ordered.

Tu'ver nodded wordlessly. His implants began to pulse with a faint light as he contacted the ship. I was beginning to like him more.

"You can't be serious," Axtin snapped.

He gave Tu'ver a small shove. Not enough to do any damage, but enough to halt the connection.

Tu'ver bared his teeth in response.

From the corner of my eye, I saw one of the females up close, the tall one with cropped hair, put her hand on her weapon.

"You object to my decision, Axtin?" I asked, keeping my voice level.

I knew the short-haired female couldn't understand the words I spoke, but she listened so intently, I could tell she was receptive to tone. The calmer I remained, the less likely I would find myself forced to "neutralize the situation." Killing civilians was not something I enjoyed doing.

"It's not just your decision when it affects our safety and the safety of the crew," Axtin argued. "Besides, babysitting injured civilians is not our job."

"It's our fault that she's been injured in the first place," Tu'ver said, his unsettling monotone way of speaking never faltering.

He was looking at the wounded woman, now struggling to sit up.

"We are at war. Casualties happen," Axtin said through gritted teeth.

As much as I hated to admit it, I would normally agree with him. But this world, these people were never meant to be involved in this war.

"Like it or not, they are valuable," I said. I could hardly believe the words coming out of my mouth. "You saw the things that live on this planet. We've never faced anything like them. We are strangers here. We don't know this world. They do."

"Oh yeah, the dying one looks really valuable," Axtin scoffed.

"She won't die," Tu'ver said coolly. "The tall one managed to work the tissue revitalizer. If we bring her to the med bay, there is no reason she wouldn't make a full recovery."

"After centuries of war, this is what you guys decide to go all buddy-buddy on?" Axtin said, running a hand through his hair.

"Try to think logically for once. I know it's difficult for your species," Tu'ver drawled.

I rolled my eyes. Nothing like barbed sarcasm to calm an irritated Valorni.

True to form, Axtin snarled at Tu'ver and shoved

him. Tu'ver's implants flared to life as he squared off in a fighting stance.

I glanced at the three females. The tallest one had lifted her weapon. Her finger rested on the trigger, but she had yet to take aim.

The blonde had moved, so that she was between us and the recovering dark-haired one. She looked ready to rip out our jugulars with her teeth.

The dark-haired one, the gentlest looking of the bunch, watched with a curious expression on her face. Like we were puzzles she was trying to solve.

"Enough!" I bellowed.

The females flinched. The tall one sat up on her knees, her weapon aimed at me once more.

I kept my eye on her, tried to convey in some way that she might understand that I had no intention of hurting any of them. At least, not for the moment.

The blonde one shouted something at the tall one that I couldn't understand. But the words appeared to make the tall one flinch. I had seen her wince like that several times already.

A negative auditory reaction, perhaps?

"They aren't part of this war. We dragged them into it, and it's our duty to protect them from the chaos the Xathi will unleash," I said.

Axtin opened his mouth to argue, but I cut him off.

"Additionally, they could have valuable information

about this world and its resources. It would be extremely foolish not to take advantage. They are coming with us. That's final."

"And you just expect them to come along willingly?" Axtin said. "They probably think we are invading their planet. Who says they won't try to kill us as soon as they get the chance?"

"If that is the case, I should think you'd be able to handle a few primitive alien females," I smirked. "Unless you think they'd be too big of a challenge."

"Fuck off," Axtin growled.

"Good, then it's decided," I clapped my hands together.

I had managed to convince my team, but the real challenge would be convincing the females. I turned to the trio with my hands up, palms facing them in an attempt to convey I wasn't a threat.

The one with the weapon considered me for a long moment before she lowered her weapon once more. The blonde hissed something to her.

"Come with us," I said slowly and gestured with my arms that they should follow.

The tall one was more adept at reading body language than the others. She seemed to understand what I was attempting to convey. She said something to the others.

The blonde reacted negatively, which I now

assumed was a regular part of the blonde's behavioral patterns.

The two began to argue, with the dark-haired one interjecting once in a while. They were gesturing wildly, looking completely ridiculous.

I might have been amused under different circumstances. But right now, they were just trying my patience.

"Their chattering is giving me a headache," Axtin said as if he had read my mind.

"Should we just grab them? We can explain everything on the ship," Tu'ver suggested.

This isn't the way I wanted to do this, but it didn't look like the females were going to come to an agreement anytime soon.

"Get the injured one," I said after a moment of consideration. "The others will likely follow without hassle."

"What about the one with the gun?" Axtin asked.

"I think she understands what we are trying to do," I replied. "Let her keep the weapon for now. You've been stunned before, right? You can handle it."

"Sure, I can handle it," Axtin snorted. "But I don't think either of you lightweights could."

"My suit is made from one of the most resilient fiber mesh alloys in the known systems," Tu'ver said. "One of those walking trees could strike me square in the chest, and it wouldn't do a hint of damage. I'm not worried about some scrappy natives with a single stun gun."

He strode over to the women, using the same open-palmed hand gesture that I had. The tall human watched him warily, but didn't raise her weapon.

Tu'ver knelt down beside the injured one.

The blonde lunged for him. She looked like she wanted to scratch his eyes out.

Axtin stepped forward, ready to grab her, but the tall one pointed her weapon at his chest.

She said something to the blonde, her teeth clenched and her frustration clear on her face. She was furious.

The injured one looked the calmest out of the three, but she was clearly uneasy with Tu'ver being so close.

Tu'ver gestured to her injury, then mimicked the movement of using the tissue revitalizer. He pointed to the mouth of the cave and then performed a ridiculous pantomime of flying a ship.

The dark-haired human considered him for a moment, before nodding slowly. The blonde shrieked in protest, and I wondered if it would be considered inhumane to muzzle her once we were back on the ship.

The dark-haired one looked at the blonde and hissed something that made the blonde go pale. Tu'ver put one arm around her back and one under her knees. He waited for her to lock her arms around his neck.

I hadn't realized K'ver were capable of being this gentle with another being. However, this wasn't the time to dwell on it.

The blonde protested once again but kept pace with Tu'ver and the dark-haired female. She struck him once in the back, but recoiled instantly. She yelped, tucking her hand against her chest.

Tu'ver really wasn't lying about his skin suit. I doubt he even knew that he'd been struck. The dark-haired one looked over his shoulder and tried to placate the blonde.

They were joined somehow, a family connection, if I had to guess.

Axtin fell in line behind the blonde. He stared daggers at the back of her head as if he was daring her to try something.

She whipped around as if he'd called out to her. She hissed something at Axtin, who only rolled his eyes.

I wondered if the moods of these creatures were reflected in their vocal patterns, or if they always sounded this discontent. If it was the latter, I was certainly in for a headache.

The tall, short-haired one refused to move. She watched the others move toward the mouth of the cave with a mixed expression that looked like worry and relief.

"You're coming, too," I said to her, knowing she wouldn't understand.

She looked at me, her expression hardening. I gestured to her then to the mouth of the cave and the others. She shook her head vehemently.

I believed that she understood we had no intention of hurting the other two, yet she didn't want to join them. She wasn't bonded to the other two in the same way the other females were bonded to each other. What an odd social dynamic.

I lifted my own blaster, not directly pointing it at her, but shifting it enough, so that she would get the idea and pointed once more to the opening of the cave. Her upper lip pulled back into a snarl as she lifted her own weapon, pointing it directly between my eyes.

Frustrated, I scrubbed at my forehead. This planet, the crash, the rift, all of it added up to one exhausted strike force leader. And for some reason, I didn't want to just leave her behind.

"Please," I growled. "I'm trying to protect you. Come with us to where it's safe."

She frowned, cocked her head like she almost understood.

But she couldn't have.

Could she?

JENEVA

"We don't know who these guys are or what they're doing here," I said again, tired of the argument that had gone on for the entire miserable hike. We'd entered an area of the jungle even I didn't venture into.

"They gave you their equipment. Would someone with bad intentions do that?" Mariella asked over the alien's shoulder.

"To gain trust, yeah."

It was no use arguing any longer. The woman had made up her mind.

My head pounded, just like it always did around people. She would jump into a raging fire to protect her sister. I couldn't fault her for that. I would do the same for my own sister, even if we didn't get along.

But these guys... From my experience, almost everyone had ulterior motives. I had no idea what to expect from them. That made my heart jump into my throat.

Other people always made me uncomfortable, ready to leave. These strangers, these aliens... felt empty.

It should have been a relief, but here I was in unknown territory, unhappy and confused.

Except, back at the cave, when it had just been me and the red one. For a flash, I'd felt something warm, safe. I'd trusted him for that moment.

Now I wasn't so sure.

Finally, we arrived at a narrow ravine. The first of the aliens slipped through, followed by the one carrying Mariella, then another.

I froze.

Didn't these idiots understand that just wandering into an unexplored, narrow area was asking something to snack on you?

Behind us, the two aliens seemed to be arguing just as much as Leena and I. Their tones were even the same. They gestured toward us too many times to count.

Finally, the green one settled down. He looked disgruntled.

The red one, obviously the leader, stood there and

looked at me expectantly. He made a choppy gesture toward the entrance.

"Nuh-uh," I said, taking a step back.

These muscle-bound maniacs could kiss my ass.

He looked impatient and gestured again.

Nope. I won't go in there.

I stuck out my chin defiantly. I'd take all the perils my jungle had to offer over that unknown hole any day.

He started talking a million miles an hour and gestured emphatically. I knew that I was being bitched out. Even Leena looked at me like I was nuts.

I grabbed the bridge of my nose, trying to press away the pain in my head.

Just shut up already!

Finally, I shrugged. I had better get an explanation when this was over. Leena and I took simultaneous steps toward the mouth of the ravine, when I stopped short and perked up my ears.

Usually, you could hear the vines creaking even when everything else was quiet. That wasn't often. It meant a predator was nearby.

The forest was eerily silent.

Then an almost inaudible whine.

"Xathi!" The red one yelled and pointed his weapon into the emptiness.

The green one stepped beside his comrade and pointed his weapon to the side.

I didn't know what *Xathi* meant, but it didn't sound good.

Leena ducked behind me as I raised my stun gun.

I wasn't sure where to aim, so I darted the thing back and forth like an idiot. I had a soft spot for the wildlife here, even if it did want to eat me most of the time. I would be pissed if I had to kill one of my creatures over a false alarm.

I heard it then. Whatever rumbled through the brush was nothing I knew. It sounded like it towered over all of us and lumbered through like a juggernaut.

The sound came from all around us.

The brawny aliens began firing. I took their lead and fired, hoping like hell I hit whatever it was and that my stunner would have any effect.

Our new friends started backing up toward us. I didn't know what the hell they were doing, so I just kept firing the weapon. It was the only thing I could think of doing.

The red one waved his hand behind him, indicating we should back up toward the ravine. It might be dangerous in there, but whatever was hiding in the jungle certainly was.

The shots coming at us seemed just as chaotic at first, but then I realized that they were calculated. Instead of one huge creature, there were a lot of them, coming fast.

I bumped into Leena as I tried to speed up my backstep. She shoved me off her. All I could do was glance back and shrug an apology.

I caught a glimpse of movement to my right.

That's all I had time for before we were surrounded.

They were like a hybrid of insect and human, ugly and mean. I tagged one with my gun while the aliens - I guess *my* aliens now - took out one after another.

We kept backing up while shooting.

The ravine entrance was still too far away to duck into. I pushed Leena in that direction with one hand and fired another shot with the other.

"Go, go, go!" I yelled.

The nasty bastard dropped like he had been deflated.

Good to know the stunner did something.

Leena tripped on her own feet, caught her balance, and sprinted for the shelter of the ravine.

Following would have been the smart thing to do. Instead, I moved forward and got closer to my new friends. We stood in a triangle, weapons pointed in different directions.

We picked off each one as it emerged from the brush. I didn't know how effective my stun gun really was, but I my aim was precise and that's the best I could do.

My reflexes had to be quick to work in the forest. I used that skill to its full advantage.

I knew our luck wouldn't last. There were too many. Eventually, they would overwhelm us.

Why the fuck didn't you run with Leena?

I shushed my inner critic and kept firing.

So far, six nasty insect-like bodies littered the ground in front of me.

We were simply outnumbered.

As soon as the first three of them charged clear of our fire, the red one yelled something. I couldn't understand the language, but I knew exactly what he said.

Run!

We split, diving behind different trees. That's all we had time for. I felt a shot buzz past as I dove.

The insect creatures blasted the wood with their weapons. I peeked around and shot at anything that moved. I wasn't even sure that I hit any of them, I had to duck behind the tree so fast.

All the while, I silently begged the tree not to take its anger and pain out on me. So far, the branches were still pointed upward, razor sharp leaves safely away. I glanced over.

The others gave no hint of moving either. They were monoliths, our only defense against the onslaught.

Fuck. There were too many of the bug creatures. They were going to overwhelm us at any moment.

I gave it two seconds before we were pulverized in the stampede. I stopped shooting and put my back against the tree. I squeezed my eyes shut and waited to die.

My tree stopped shaking under the onslaught. I only pictured the blood-like sap oozing from its trunk on the other side and briefly wondered if they could die. I glanced over, and the other two looked as confused as me.

Then I heard it.

The telltale creaking of the vines, the lumbering of sorvuc. I could swear I heard some of the animals growling in the distance.

My forest, my home, had just become creepy.

All right. Creepier.

A quick glance around the tree confirmed my suspicions. I didn't know if insect creatures were supposed to be capable of looking terrified, but they certainly did. Their six eyes darted all over the place, and their six legs trembled.

Even Green and Red stopped firing when they saw the flora come to life. They didn't look terrified. They looked intrigued.

Idiots.

The vines were quicker than our attackers gave

them credit for. They wound their way around appendages while the sorvuc surrounded them.

The vines tightened and pulled, toppling the insect creatures. Others slithered in and disarmed them while they were bound.

I didn't know how long it would take before the living wood changed their minds about killing me, too. When I saw three sorvuc ambling in our direction, it was my turn. Those bastards were living weapons waiting for war.

"Run!" I yelled at Red and Green.

I didn't wait. I sprinted toward the ravine and dove in.

In diving, though, I lost my grip on my stun gun. I watched it clatter against the rocks, the cheap construction shattering into at least two dozen useless pieces of shrapnel.

I was defenseless.

My new friends were right behind me as I jumped to my feet. I looked around them, expecting to be pursued by trees, vines, or insect creatures. What I saw astounded me.

The sorvuc lined up beside their shot-to-hell kin. Their branches entwined together and filled the gaps between the trunks, making a barrier between us and the insect creatures.

In a million years, I would never have guessed that

the forest life would want to protect me.

Red chattered something and spun me around. My mouth dropped open.

The ravine twisted before me for a few more yards, then was blocked by a massive... something.

Aliens.

Had to get here by a ship, right?

Hell.

At the end of the passage stood an industrial-looking door, leading into the craft.

I planted my feet, myths and legends of gory experiments racing through my head.

Red nudged me forward. I stumbled a little, fear getting the better of me. He nudged again, this time with exasperated chatter.

No. I wasn't moving. Not without some assurances.

Looking even more exasperated, Red grumbled to himself. Then he reached to his belt and handed me a wicked looking blaster.

Pausing a moment, I took it.

The heft was good. And I could tell it would certainly do some damage.

Good. Now I had no problem following my new "friends".

I reluctantly advanced.

The door slid up and we stepped through.

VREHX

Zairk, our resident medic, wanted to take the injured female to the med bay, but Tu'ver wouldn't hand her over.

"Carry her, then, for all I care. Less stress on me." Zairk's exasperation was palpable, then again, he was always exasperated about something.

As Tu'ver left with Zairk, the blonde female followed after, leaving the one that I had given the weapon to. I wanted to talk to her, but I needed to speak with Rouhr first.

However, Axtin, Daxion, and Sakev stood before me, faces grim.

With a tilt of my head, I took in a deep breath and let it out slowly.

Waiting.

If they wanted to say something, the first move was theirs.

Axtin, of course, charged in. "We're giving the natives weapons now?"

Sakev cut him off with a frown. "What if she tries to shoot us?"

"You think she's going to be able to reprogram the protocols?" The weapons wouldn't fire on board a Skotan ship. Kept everyone from being killed by a rookie drilling a hole in the hull.

Axtin chuckled a bit. "Yeah, messes with my practice time. But seriously, why'd you give her the weapon? Could have just had me and Sakev come back out to help make Xathi jewelry."

"She's a better shot than you. She did more damage with her toy gun than you srelled with your blasters."

That drew a laugh from the team, even from Axtin himself. The damn behemoth was enjoying this. Then his eyes hardened. "Any idea why they sent out that many of the scouts? I don't think I remember them sending that many out at once so early in an attack."

"Not sure, but let's not worry about it too much for now. What are we going to do with these three?"

Axtin shrugged and looked at the others, who shook their heads. "Not my department. I'm just the muscle.

You're the leader that hands out weapons to the indigenous life."

The three of them laughed as they headed off. I motioned for the other female to follow me.

As we entered the lift, I watched her, her softness hiding such strength of will. Interesting.

She still clung to the blaster I gave her, and I could tell she was trying not to look at me, the same as I was trying not to look at her. The ride up the three levels to the captain's room was quick, but not fast enough that I didn't feel awkward, uncomfortable.

Nothing that a Skotan warrior should feel.

As the doors opened, I led her to the captain's small ready room off the bridge.

Rouhr was using the view screen on the wall to look over reports on the engine and the ship's power cells. The section of the ship that held the experimental weapon looked odd, blanked out.

Not my problem, not now.

"Talk to me, Vrehx."

I gestured for the female to sit down.

"We may have a problem, Captain."

"I saw. The Xathi are breaking pattern. They must be desperate to get off the planet."

"That's what I'm thinking. They're searching for something."

He let out a sigh. It was odd to see him look so old, so overwhelmed, but I thought I understood. We were in a galaxy we didn't know, on a planet no one'd ever heard of, fighting the Xathi, and apparently fighting the damn planet, as well.

Not to mention the fact that the ship was broken. "Any clues what they might be looking for?"

I thought about it for a few seconds, but the only thing that came to my mind were the basics.

"Food, fuel, information. Probably the same as us."

He nodded. "What about her and her friends?"

"I don't know. One had been severely injured by the local wildlife when we found them. I made the tactical decision to help, then brought them along, hoping that we can get some information from them."

"I see that she's holding one of your blasters," he commented blandly.

Dammit, not him too. I nodded and thankfully he didn't continue along those lines.

"Have you tried talking to her?"

"Not exactly. We couldn't communicate outside and haven't exactly had a moment to speak yet since we've boarded the ship."

"Really?" He smiled at me as he took a seat. "You've been around this woman for however long now, were alone together on the lift, and you haven't even tried?"

"No, sir."

He cocked his head.

I felt my blood rise as he turned to her, began talking, trusting the ship's translation programs to take care of the language barrier.

Something about her made my heart race, made me uneasy. I didn't have to understand it, I just had to do my job. She was a tool, nothing more.

I tried to slow my breathing and concentrated on their conversation.

There wasn't much of one.

"I can't understand a thing she says."

I tried.

"Can you tell us your name?"

She looked at me and said...something. I couldn't tell what it was, it was all "wanh wanh, wanh wanh" to me. It was like trying to listen to someone with a speech impediment using a broken microphone.

I wondered what I sounded like to her.

Rouhr and I looked at one another.

"Now what?"

His question mirrored my own thoughts.

She was still talking, trying to tell us something.

I held up my hand, trying to motion for her to wait a second. I went over to the computer panel and got into the translation program. I double checked everything, trying to make sure everything was turned on and working properly.

A few things seemed off, so I restarted the program and made sure everything was turned on.

When it came on, we tried again.

"Can you tell us your name and where we are?"

It didn't work. She looked just as frustrated and angry as I felt.

"So, we can't talk to her. We can't find out where we are and what we're dealing with. Ideas?"

I sat back in the chair and thought. There was something. It was archaic, and not the greatest way to endear yourself to the other person, but it was better than this impasse.

"I have an idea, but it's going to be a bad one."

He looked at me, saw the chagrin on my face, and put his head in his hands.

"You have *got* to be kidding me. You're telling me we have the pattern for one of those damn things on board?"

"You can thank your medic, he's the one with the weird historical collection."

"You know that it could hurt her, right?"

"What choice do we have, Captain? We don't have a clue about anything on this damn rock, and the only people we can talk to can't understand us. Do you have any other ideas?"

At the shake of his head, I got into the computer archives and started looking for what I needed. After finding it, I put in the request, and the program fired up. If this worked, we'd be able to talk to the natives and finally figure out what the hell was going on here.

If she didn't hate me for doing it.

JENEVA

They were trying to communicate with me, I think. It was hard to tell. A lot of gesturing, definitely some frustration.

But for all I knew, they were debating how best to kill and eat me. I fingered the trigger of the blaster that had been given to me. I wasn't sure exactly how it worked, but from the feel of it, it sure did pack a much harder punch than my old stun gun.

I was tempted to fire it, to cause a distraction or even a minor injury, and make my escape. However, that didn't seem like a particularly wise plan. If they didn't want me dead now, they likely would if I attempted to open fire on them.

And I was hilariously outnumbered.

I watched the two aliens, hardly daring to blink for

fear that I would miss some small clue alluding to the nature of their conversation. Well, it was really more like an argument.

The pair was looking at a computer. My alien—well, not *mine*, the one that brought me to this ship, spoke in low tones to another alien that must have been of the same species. They both had red-toned skin with those retractable scales.

But the other one looked...older. It was difficult to put it into words. His coloring was as bold as my alien's, but there was something in his movements and the way he carried himself.

A scar marred his face. He wore his experience like a badge.

I caught the eye of my alien. He was frowning. I kept my face an expressionless mask until he looked back to the computer.

He typed something in, and the machine began to whirl and hum. In front of the pair, a very small laser-like device pointed its beam on the desk. It jerked back and forth rapidly.

Something materialized where the beam was pointed. He picked up the small object, a small white pill, and extended his hand to me.

I hesitated before taking the pill.

"What is it?" I asked even though I knew they wouldn't understand.

I lifted my hand to my mouth and mimicked the motion of swallowing. From the panicked look on their faces, that wasn't what they wanted me to do.

My alien pointed to the pill in my hand then pointed to the side of my head.

"You want me to put this…in my ear?"

He repeated the motion, smirked a little bit. I narrowed my eyes before pushing the pill into my ear canal.

At first, nothing happened. Then I felt it. Like an insect with a thousand legs, it wriggled and burrowed deeper into my ear canal.

I felt it scratch along my brain. It nipped and pinched.

I clawed at my ear, desperate to make it stop. Sinking to my knees, I fumbled for the blaster, but I only managed to drop it on the metal floor.

I wasn't aware that I'd screamed until my throat started to ache. Arms wrapped around me, but it wasn't until I saw red skin that I reacted.

"Don't touch me! Make it stop!" I screamed.

I attempted to thrash, but found myself wholly restrained.

"Easy," a voice said.

A voice! I could understand them.

"It will be over momentarily." And just like that, the pain was gone.

It was as if nothing had happened. I took a shuddering breath and leaned against something solid and warm.

For a moment, I let myself relax, then it snapped. I shoved him away and struggled to stand on my own. "What the hell was that?" I demanded.

"It's a small device that tracks the neural patterns in your brain when you speak," the alien explained as if he were explaining a technical manual. "It then transmits those patterns to the computer, which translates them and broadcast them to nearby devices in the network."

"So, I can understand you and you can understand me?"

"Plainly," he said with a look of disdain I would have slapped off if I weren't sure the aliens surrounding me wouldn't put me down for it.

"You shove a brain reading device into my head and now you're giving me attitude?" I settled for being snarky.

I felt like I was owed that much after everything that had happened today.

"I didn't shove it into your brain," he argued.

"You told me to shove it into my brain, knowing I had no idea what to expect!" I snapped back.

"Even the simplest life form could have predicted—"

"Enough," the other alien, the older one, grumbled.

My alien went ramrod straight in perfect attention.

"We have bigger problems," the older one continued. He turned to me.

"I am General Rouhr, Captain of this vessel, the *Vengeance*. I am of the Skotan race, as is Vrehx."

He jerked his chin in the direction of the alien that had brought me here.

Vrehx. I turned the name over in my mind. *Skotan.*

"I'm Jeneva of the human race," I said uneasily. "The other humans are Mariella and Leena. Where are they?"

"The injured one has been taken to the med bay, and as far as I know, the other one has refused to leave the injured one's side," the General explained.

"They're sisters," I said blankly, but I immediately regretted my words.

I didn't know if I should have given up their information just like that. I still didn't know why these Skotan were here or what they wanted.

"Yes, Vrehx mentioned that the pair were likely joined by a family bond," the General mused.

"Yes," I said because, frankly, I didn't know how else to respond.

There was a tense silence that lasted several heartbeats.

"What...what happened?" I asked. "The sky tore open. The animals in the forest went berserk, and then you showed up."

I threw a pointed look at Vrehx.

"Vrehx, I'll let you explain this one," the General said with a heavy tone.

Vrehx rubbed the back of his neck and sighed.

"My people, as well as several others," he nodded to the various alien beings buzzing around the bridge outside the door, "are allies in a war. We were in combat when a powerful weapon malfunctioned on a catastrophic level. That's what caused the rift to open. That's how we came to be here."

Vrehx's eyes quickly locked with General Rouhr's before quickly looking away.

"What else?" I asked, my eyes narrowed.

"Pardon?" Vrehx asked.

"There's more to it than that. Tell me," I insisted.

Vrehx hesitated.

"It's her world, Vrehx," General Rouhr sighed. "She should know exactly what sort of danger this planet is in."

"The enemy we are fighting, the Xathi, also came through the rift," he said.

"What the hell are the Xathi?" I asked, not caring that my voice was getting louder with each word.

"You saw them outside," Vrehx explained. "Anything outside of the hive is considered either a hostile or a resource. They have no tolerance or respect for any other life form."

Aliens.

Fine, ok. When our colony ship arrived here, *we* were aliens. So I could almost handle that.

Alien ship. I guess. Alien technology. Made sense, once I got past the whole aliens thing.

A war falling through the sky and onto my home?

My brain blanked for a moment.

And what about the weapon Vrehx mentioned? It was horrible enough that a genocidal hive-minded alien race even existed in the first place, but if they had technology powerful enough to punch clean into another universe, how could we ever hope to stop them?

"What are you going to do about it?" I demanded.

"Only a single Xathi ship fell through the rift. Those onboard will likely be separated from the hive-mind. We believe it will make them unstable, likely more aggressive. However, they will be more disorganized. It's there that we may have an advantage," Vrehx explained.

"That doesn't sound like an advantage to me," I said. "A creature is at its most dangerous when it's wounded and in distress. They will do anything, even mutilate themselves, to ensure survival. I doubt these Xathi are an exception."

"You know much about the animals of this world?"

I nodded. "You learn a lot when you live out in the middle of nowhere for fifteen years," I shrugged.

I really didn't feel like digging into my past with the Skotan.

"Your knowledge could be invaluable to us," Vrehx replied. "In fact, your potential wealth of information about this world is why the Valorni and the K'ver agreed with me in bringing you onto the ship."

Valorni. K'ver.

I assumed those were the races of the other two aliens that were in the cave with us.

"What do you need to know?" I asked, warily.

I still didn't trust Vrehx. Or anyone aboard this ship. For all I knew, they could be lying about everything in order to exploit the information I gave them.

"The Xathi will target the largest remaining city first. They will strip it of resources. The civilians they allow to live will become their slaves. Once they have taken all they can use, they will move on to the surrounding towns," Vrehx explained. "We need to know everything possible about this world so that we can plot a defense."

"My sister," I almost choked, my heart speeding up so fast I thought it was going to leap straight out of my chest. I brought a hand to my throat as if I could force myself to breathe normally. From the corner of my eye, I saw Vrehx reach toward me but then he seemed to think better of it.

"My sister lives in Kaster. I have to go get her!" I

patted my sides, looking for that stupid blaster Vrehx had given me.

"Out of the question," Vrehx said, crossing his arms over his chest.

"I'm not leaving her there to be enslaved by hostile aliens!" There it was. I scooped it up from the floor, clutching the blaster tight.

Vrehx turned to General Rouhr. "We need a more complete recon mission anyway," he said. "Why don't I take my team? We can scout the area and bring back Jeneva's sister."

"No way in hell," I scoffed. "I don't trust you. Amira sure as shit isn't going to trust you. Hell, Amira doesn't even trust me."

The words left a bitter taste on my tongue.

"It's the only option," Vrehx argued.

I palmed my weapon. I wasn't sure how it worked, but I didn't need details right now.

"No, it's not," I said, turning back to face Vrehx, and held the weapon triumphantly. "You're going to take me with you."

VREHX

The wild, fierce look stayed on her face even as she headed towards the exit, a weapon she had no idea how to use clutched in her upraised hand. Srell, there would be no end to the recked teasing now.

With my best no-nonsense expression in place, I stared stoically back at the bridge crew. Not one of them had the decency to wipe the smirk from his face.

I focused on Rouhr instead, hoping he, at least, wouldn't mention the damn weapon.

"I think it would serve us to accompany her."

"Is that so?"

"She's our best shot at learning something about this planet. And if she stumbled across the Xathi on her own, you know she wouldn't be coming back."

Rouhr raised a hand to his chin in thought; it was all

I could do not to bounce with impatience. Any second now, she'd figure out how to open the door and work the lift, and then we might never catch up to her. Not in this unfamiliar terrain.

For some reason, the thought bothered me.

"Very well," Rouhr finally announced, the words barely out of his mouth before I was at her side.

"Wait," I demanded, grabbing her arm. The touch of her skin sparked a heat in my chest. I pulled back quickly, rubbing my hand absently. "My team and I will come with you."

The look of victory was back on her face, her eyes shone at me. "What are we waiting for, let's go." Her anxiety was damn near palpable.

"We'll just need a moment to prepare."

Minutes later, the six of us stepped from the ship back into the ravine, the men looking around cautiously. We'd already encountered our fair share of surprises on this planet, not one of us wanted any more.

At our waists, we now wore holographic belts, each hastily programmed with human traits and modified for generalized male characteristics. One press of a button and we were indistinguishable from the rest of the dominant race on this planet.

We hoped.

Jeneva looked us each over in turn, her eyes seeming

to linger longer once they reached me.

"Well?" I asked, glancing down at my own disguise.

She started slightly, her eyes pulled back to my face.

"It'll do."

With that, she turned, starting off on a path only visible in her mind.

We hurried to follow, and I quickly ordered the men into a defensive formation around her. She was our only source of information on this new planet; we had to keep her safe.

At least, that's the reason I gave myself for wanting to protect her.

She looked at us skeptically as we encircled her, a single brow rising as we moved into place.

"What the hell are you doing?" she asked, looking blankly at me.

"Defensive formation."

"I don't need your *defense*."

Her defiance, while amusing, was the last thing I needed just then; least of all in front of the men.

"I am the leader of this strike team." Anger crackled through my voice. "If you want to travel with us, you will have to listen to my orders, just as the men do."

She tilted her head and laughed, "Then I suppose I don't want to travel with you."

Srell.

I took a step forward and forced my expression to remain blank.

"You do not want to go up against the Xathi alone. You have no idea what you're dealing with."

"And you have no idea where you are. I'd say that's a pretty big handicap."

I heard a chuckle from among the men, muffled but audible.

"You are making this very difficult." I said, ignoring the men and focusing on the issue at hand—Jeneva.

"Oh darn, well, let me make it less so. Goodbye."

With that she turned, forced her way between the men, and walked quickly away from us.

"Shouldn't have given her a weapon," Tu'ver offered, a smirk pulling at his lips.

It had only been a matter of time.

"I don't want to hear it," I growled, heading after the now rogue human.

"Wait!" I called, forcing the word out in the form of an order.

She spun, the weapon clenched in her hand now pointed towards my head.

"I think I've heard enough orders," she said and took a step forward. "Now I'm going to find my sister. *Alone.* You can do whatever you like."

I stepped forward quickly, plucked the weapon easily from her grasp.

"Hey!" she shouted, and reached out in a too slow attempt to reclaim it.

"You don't even know how to use it."

"I was gonna figure it out! Besides, you really want me to be unarmed against the Xath—whatever?"

"Xathi. And no, I want you to stop being defiant and let us escort you, as I said we would."

She grumbled and looked down. "Fine."

I located the small switch hidden in the weapon's grip and quickly flicked it upward. I was immediately rewarded with the faint hum of a now-active weapon.

She watched me stoically and bit her lip in irritation.

I brought it to my waist, intending to holster it for myself, but hesitated. I would never hear the end of it, that was for sure, but something stopped me.

With a sigh, I extended my arm again, offering the weapon. Surprise flashed across her face, quickly replaced with a smile. Slowly, she reclaimed it.

"Thank you."

A surge seemed to pass through me at her words, at her smile.

I smothered it quickly, turning to wave the men to us. The moment they reached us, all eyes turned to the now-active blaster.

"Srell," Tu'ver exclaimed. "Again, Vrehx?"

I ignored him, gestured for Jeneva to lead the way.

We walked in silence for several minutes, the men occasionally glanced towards Jeneva's upheld weapon, only to turn to me with mixed expressions. Somehow, I found it hard to care.

Without her own weapon, Jeneva was a target; a thought I didn't much care for.

I walked beside her, easily kept pace with her hurried steps. Since defensive formation hadn't gone over so well, I chose not to try my luck twice. Still, I wasn't about to leave her side.

After a few more minutes of silence, I glanced in her direction. Her eyes swayed from side to side and inspected our surroundings with great attention. It was a look I knew well from the battlefield.

Something wasn't right.

"What is it?" I asked, slowing my stride.

She slowed along with me, glanced over the surrounding trees before she focused on me.

"It's too quiet."

I glanced around in turn, keenly aware of my own lack of knowledge about this land. "You think something's wrong?"

"I know it is."

With that, she was off again, eyes raking over our surroundings. I followed close, tried my best to look for signs of disturbance.

We came upon the outpost stealthily, despite

Jeneva's desire to hurry. I smelled the smoke before we even set eyes on the place, and I knew.

The Xathi were already gone, our only stroke of luck on what turned out to be a grim day. Around us, fires still sputtered, but the structures that fed them were already burnt to husks. Bodies littered the ground, blood flowed like a stream down the slight incline of the hill.

To our right lay the smoking remains of a Xathi sled, it's large, V-shaped frame dented and crushed from impact. One entry door had almost entirely detached, it now hung crooked in the frame, giving view to a darkened interior.

Jeneva stood wide-eyed at my side, her mouth slightly agape in the face of the slave transport vehicle.

"It's okay," I said, trying for a reassuring tone, "they're long gone."

"Monsters," she finally managed, her voice husky with emotion.

"Yes," I agreed, "monsters."

The sight brought back memories too painful to touch; I shoved them violently away.

Jeneva swayed slightly, her hand moved to her head as if she were pained.

"We have to go help the survivors." She surged forward.

I reached out to grab her arm, stilled her.

"There won't be any."

"There are," she said simply, and tried again to move forward.

"Listen to me, there are no survivors. I know how the Xathi work. I've seen it before. They like to set an example early."

She shook me off, swayed again, "You're wrong."

I sighed as she rushed into the narrow road between buildings. I understood her denial; it was only natural in the face of so much death.

But I'd been here before. I already knew.

After a second of debate, I followed after her and gestured for the men to come along. They spoke to each other in hushed whispers, not that there was anyone around to bother with their talk.

We followed Jeneva to a collapsed building, one of the few spared from the fire. With some difficulty, we managed to force our way inside.

"This way," she said and pointed towards the back of the building, the side still mostly erect.

We walked in silence, our way of paying respect. Halfway through the space, the first sound caught my ear: soft moans. The men grew instantly alert, their attention drawn to the sounds.

Now we hurried, our boots kicking up dust as we rushed toward the noise. Jeneva led the way, nervous energy making her stumble as she ran.

We found them against a far wall; the few unlucky survivors, each worse than the last. The floorboards here were drenched with blood, great pools that rippled as we stepped forward.

The air was heavy with the scent of imminent death.

Jeneva stood where the blood trails intersected, her hand on her head, her skin noticeably paler.

"There's nothing we can do for them." I said and stopped by her side.

"Of course, we can *do* something," she said through gritted teeth, "we have to help them!"

"There is no help for them."

I looked at the poor creatures, mutilated bodies unable to do more than whimper. Past what even our med bay, with all of its technology, could heal.

I turned to Tu'ver, nodded my head slightly as our eyes met. He didn't speak, just nodded in turn.

His weapon was in his hand in an instant, his aim true. Before Jeneva could even process what was happening, they were all gone, their suffering at an end.

"Wha—" she started, "no!"

"Jeneva…"

Her legs gave way and she collapsed to her knees, blood quickly soaking the thin fabric of her clothes.

"What did you do? We were supposed to help them!" Both of her hands cradled her head, her body shook.

"They couldn't be helped; all that was left for them was pain. It wasn't right to let them suffer."

Panting, each lungful of her air sounded strained.

I turned to Axtin, inclined my head towards the shocked human who trembled at my feet.

He nodded and stepped forward slowly.

"Let me take you out of here," he said, laying a hand on her shoulder.

She nodded once, took a deep breath, and stood. Then, leaning on him, she shuffled from the room. I watched them go, my mind turning.

I hadn't expected Jeneva to react well when we euthanized members of her species, but for her to seem so pained? It bothered me to watch her suffer, even more than it had to see the other humans do the same.

This female. She was a mysterious one.

And somehow, I was going to figure her out.

JENEVA

I allowed myself one glance at Vrehx before I returned my gaze straight ahead.

He'd taken the massacre in stride.

Hell. He'd added to the body count.

Tu'ver had a hint of emotion on his face as he killed the survivors. But he'd done it anyway.

Were the men I travelled with any better than the alleged bad guys?

Wasn't killing still killing, whatever your motive?

I could still hear the screams of the dying in my mind. Maybe it had been mercy, after all.

But they hadn't even tried...

Images of smoke, dead bodies, and flames licking at general rubble overlaid my vision.

And something else haunted me. If I didn't get to my sister before the Xathi, that could be her fate.

We travelled quickly, the men keeping up with me better than I'd expected. No one that big had any right to move so quietly.

Axtin stayed slightly ahead of me and Vrehx, scouting, checking back with me for signals on the path. Vrehx stayed closer, nearly beside me, so close I couldn't help but be aware of his presence, his strength. It was strange to have someone watch over me.

Almost… nice.

"Tell me the rules of this place," Vrehx said softly.

I frowned. "Rules? What do you mean?"

Maybe he was trying to distract me from worrying about Amira, but that wasn't happening.

"Surely you have a book of rules people study to live by and abide by?"

What was he suggesting? A rule book of our planet? It was the most absurd idea I'd heard in a long time.

"What for?"

It was not as if the creatures in the jungle would read them. Wouldn't be bad if we could make them.

"For law and order. So everyone knows." Vrehx stopped, eyes narrowed.

"There's no rule book," I told him, not hiding my impatience from my voice. "It's about blending and getting on with other species."

I pointed toward Axtin. "See how he blends?"

From Vrehx's furrowed brow, I could tell this had not been my best example. "Because he's green." He almost spat the words.

I shook my head. "It's more than that. See how he moves? Our planet is about working out how to live with what we have. How to survive without killing everything. Axtin blends in by the way he moves. He's trying to become one with the flora."

Vrehx shook his head. His jaw tightened, and it might have been my imagination, but I thought his skin glowed a little redder.

"Told you," Axtin turned toward us.

"I mean--" I realized sparks were about to fly between the two men if I didn't step in. What sort of team was this? "You'll work out pretty quickly which plants kill, and which ones only scare."

Tu'ver came up beside me. "You have plants who've combined with animals, is that right?"

I nodded. "It seems that a partnership has developed between them. Take the boab tree. It has vines with buds. The buds are the houses for the flying dragon creature. Any food they catch between them, they share. It's a win-win situation."

I heard Vrehx growl but couldn't make out his words.

Before any more could be said on the subject, I

stopped dead in my tracks. Before us stretched out the city my sister lived in.

It looked nothing like the small, bustling city I remembered.

There were no sounds except for the occasional scream. The streets were still, lined with burning buildings, flattened houses, and scorched earth.

The drumming of my pulse in my ears almost drowned out the nausea that bent me over.

Almost.

So much pain.

And somewhere in that was Amira.

She could be dead. Likely was. More than likely.

But... like a small beacon through the haze of confusion in my head, I could almost feel her.

Blind optimism?

Detached from reality?

Didn't know, didn't care.

She was out there, and I was going to find her.

"Jeneva," someone spoke to me.

The voice didn't penetrate the cloak of feelings wrapped tightly around me. It was only when two hands shook me by the shoulders I looked up at Vrehx.

"Jeneva, look at me. You need to focus. The city has been attacked. The chances of her..."

"No. You're wrong," I cut him off.

I tried to keep my voice under control, didn't want to sound hysterical. "She's alive."

I watched him shake his head.

"Look, you don't understand. You don't know these Xathi as well as we do. Whoever survived will wish they hadn't. The elders and injured will be used for meat for young Xathi." He swallowed, looked away. "The women to breed more meat."

"She's alive." I pushed away. No point wasting any more time. I needed to get to her. I needed to find her, now.

"Jeneva," Vrehx forced me to look at him. "Please, you won't find her down there. And if you do-"

I pushed his hand away. "You were wrong before."

His lips tightened into a thin line. "Axtin, Tu'ver. Scout ahead. Find us a way into that recking city that won't get us spotted."

As we got closer, I caught sight of bodies in a cage. Arms, legs, and heads poked through the bars, a crush of limbs from so many captured.

My head felt as if it was about to explode.

"Do you see her?" Vrehx whispered behind me.

I didn't respond, dragging my attention from the first cage to another. More captives, more terror.

The vice around my temples tightened.

Vrehx touched my back, and I leaned into his touch.

"To have any chance of rescuing them, we need to get to them before the Xathi load them onto their ship."

My eyes glued onto the wire cages until they hurt from the strain.

Vrehx said something else, but I didn't hear it.

I'd spotted her.

"There," my voice barely sounded like my own. "She's there."

As I focused on her, I realized the prisoners in the cage in front of hers had begun to shuffle forward.

The loading process had begun.

VREHX

A small space had been cleared in the middle of what used to be an intersection. We could smell the smoke from the burning city around us as the Xathi began to load people.

Damn.

Jeneva let out a small gasp and began to move forward, out from behind the section of wall we were all hiding behind.

"Wait," I hissed as I grabbed her arm. She glared at me.

She was afraid for her sister. I got that.

She was angry at the Xathi for hurting her and her people. I understood the feeling.

But the rage in her eyes seemed to be directed at me.

That disturbed me more than it should have.

"If we rush in, we're dead, and that won't help her. They have a hive-mind. The instant *one* knows of us, they *all* know of us."

I turned to Daxion. "Dax? How many of them are you seeing?"

Daxion crept forward, being careful to stay hidden. He was back in only a few seconds. "Ten Xathi in total. Three hunters, seven soldiers."

Jeneva's whisper cut in as I nodded. "How can you tell who are hunters or who are soldiers?"

"Their coloring. The black ones are hunters. They're the ones who search for food and hunt it down. The blue ones are the soldiers. They're more dangerous because of their brute strength, but the black ones are fast and silent, making them dangerous in their own right. They're more likely to run than fight with the soldiers there."

She gnawed her lip. "And because of the hive-mind thing, all the Xathi everywhere will know we're here?"

I nodded to her, then used hand signals to disperse the team. Axtin headed out to the left with Tu'ver, while Sakev and Daxion snuck off to our right.

Looking at Jeneva's drawn face, I tried to summon a calming smile. "It'll be simple. Stay behind me, shoot the Xathi, and if you get a chance to let the prisoners free, get them out of here. We'll handle the rest."

She dropped her head to focus on the weapon I'd given her and swallowed hard. The slight shake in her hands revealed how terrified she was, but she nodded her head. Not the confident nod of a soldier, but the scared shitless nod of someone entering their first real fight.

I put my hand under her chin and lifted her face up, smoothing my thumb along her cheek. "Just stay low and wait for your chance. Be fast."

With that, I turned away from her to check my surroundings. Ten feet in front of me was a piece of roofing...not quite big enough to hide me, but big enough to be used.

The Xathi were concentrating on their prey, and none of them were looking in our direction, so I made my way out into the open just a few feet, positioning myself behind the piece of roof.

Trusting the others were where they needed to be, I took aim at a hunter, shooting at the joint where the front leg connected to the body. Taking out that leg threw off their balance, making them clumsy when they went in the direction of the missing limb.

Don't miss.

I pulled the trigger, then dove back behind the wall with Jeneva. Sneaking a peek, I could see that my aim had been true. By all that was holy, I actually hit the joint on my first shot. The others began opening fire from their positions.

Axtin, not even bothering to hide his position as he unloaded with his blaster, barely missed the humans in the process. Tu'ver was more precise, no humans were in line with any of his blasts as he shot from a second-floor window. Sakev managed to pop another limb off the Xathi that I had hit, while Daxion jumped on the back of one of the soldiers and shot it point blank in the back of the head. Pieces of crystalline shell filled the air around him.

In the two seconds since I fired, one hunter was down while the rest of the Xathi were already moving to defend. Daxion's opponent reared up on its hind legs, throwing him off, while the other six soldiers quickly dispersed. Axtin switched weapons as three of the Xathi advanced, the clickety-clack of their "feet" ricocheting off the walls of the buildings around us.

The other three soldiers spread out after Sakev and Daxion. As for the two remaining hunters, they had begun climbing the building towards Tu'ver's window.

"Tu'ver! Two hunters coming your way. Get out," I ordered as I fired at the hunters, trying to dislodge them, or, at least, distract them long enough for Tu'ver to escape.

Feeling a slight bit of satisfaction as the hunters stopped climbing to look toward me, I shifted my attention to Daxion and Sakev. Sakev led one of the soldiers into an alleyway while Daxion swung his rifle like a club. I ran over, firing along the way, and hit Daxion's first target, causing it to crack. Then, as it took another step, half of its head fell off.

If I had time to sit and watch, it would have been interesting to see the blue bug stumble, tangling in its own legs, and fall, breaking the rest of the head on the pavement. But I was too busy emptying my blaster into the second bug attacking Daxion. It had managed to get Dax's arm between its mandibles, and blood dripped from its jaws.

A roar of frustration from Axtin came from behind me, but my concentration was on Dax. Another few seconds, and the Xathi's "teeth" would grind his arm off. I wrapped my arms around the Xathi's head, grabbed the outside of each mandible, and pulled. Only a fraction of an inch, but it was enough for Daxion to pull his arm out, blood pouring from the mouth of the Xathi.

Daxion used his off-hand to grab his second blaster, shoved it into the throat of the Xathi and fired off six shots. I felt the impact and shake of the bug as it died, the dead weight of the creature yanking me to my knees before I could let go.

Sakev was at Daxion's side, helping him bind his arm. He nodded behind me and I turned to see Axtin wrestling with a soldier, its middle legs scratching and cutting his body. He had a grip on each half of the Xathi's mouth, was pulling with all his incredible strength. I unslung my rifle and took aim, pulling the trigger at the same moment he ripped the creature's head in half. He shot me a salute, broke off a leg from the dead bug, then used it as a club to beat on another one.

Tu'ver was hanging out another window, sniping at the two hunters, breaking off tiny pieces and parts with each shot. *Where was the last soldier?*

Jeneva's scream cut through my chest and I spun back towards the Xathi transport.

She was on the ground, holding her arm while trying to back away from the last soldier. Her blaster was on the ground, yards away. The Xathi snapped and clacked its jaws together.

Suddenly I was on top of the bug, pummeling and pounding on it. A broken piece of the transport unit was clenched in my fist as I stabbed and crushed the soldier.

When Axtin grabbed my arm and stopped me from swinging my make-shift weapon again, there were only a few pieces of the Xathi left, none of them any bigger than my foot.

My breath came hard and fast and my mind reeled, trying to catch up.

What the hell had happened?

Daxion and Sakev, still across the street, stared at me with jaws dropped. Tu'ver mumbled to himself as he helped Jeneva to her feet.

The look she gave me made me wish I could read her mind.

Axtin's chuckle brought me back to reality.

"Skr-r-r-r-e-e-l! And I thought you guys were the serious, rule followers. Didn't know we had another berserker race to play with!" He laughed deeply as he let go of my arm. His laugh was infectious as Tu'ver and Sakev joined in. Daxion flashed me a smile and a headshake.

"What do you mean?"

"Whoa! Easy, Vrehxy, easy," Axtin rumbled as he put his hands in the air as a sign of mock surrender., then lifted his left arm to show me a nasty bruise forming near his elbow. "Even got me a couple times before I could grab your arm."

Couldn't be.

My race didn't lose control. *I* didn't lose control. Yet I'd done exactly that; I'd lost control...in front of my men, and in front of Jeneva. She still looked at me like I was a monster.

Fine.

We had a job to do anyway.

"Next time, don't get your arm in my way," I

growled at Axtin. "Let's deal with these people. Tu'ver! Quick recon. Make sure no more Xathi are nearby. Sakev, help Jeneva open the doors, and let those prisoners out. Axtin, reload, just in case we're not done fighting. Let's *move!*"

But the fear in Jeneva's eyes still haunted me.

JENEVA

Movement and color came at me from every direction. Blood-stained faces, hysterical women, and broken men clustered around me.

All I wanted to do was run and hide.

All they wanted was reassurance, but I was the wrong person.

Blood dripped from the gash in my arm inflicted by the Xathi, and the pressure on my head, the sickness in my gut, intensified the closer the survivors pressed towards me.

All I wanted was Amira.

But alone of the crowd, she hadn't come closer. If anything, she'd stepped back, eyes hard and narrow.

It was hard to make a way through the mass of humans crowding around me. I wasn't quite sure why they ignored the men, yet bombarded me with questions.

I'd come to town as often as I could to check on Amira, to make sure her school fees were paid, then later to help find her new apartment, pay as many of her expenses as I could.

But I hadn't met that many people in town, had I?

A hideous thought struck and I whirled to check on the team.

No, their holographic disguises were still in place. They just looked… big. Dangerous.

But human enough.

"Jeneva, what's going on?" asked another person I didn't recognize.

There were too many questions thrown my way. I decided to ignore them all.

I shoved those too close to me out of the way. It was all about priorities. Right now, my priority was my sister.

When I reached her, I threw my good arm around her to pull her close to me. She resisted. Instead of returning the embrace Amira's body stiffened and she freed herself from my arms.

"Where were you?" she spat the words at me. "Somewhere else. Like always."

Open-mouthed, I watched the way she folded her

arms in front of her chest and stuck out her chin, the way a five-year-old did if they didn't get their way.

"Amira, I was," I stumbled over my words. I hadn't expected her to be this hostile when I found her.

All my energies had been focused on finding her. Now that I had, I had to deal with an entirely different problem.

Crap.

"Do you have any idea what it's been like..." she stopped in mid-sentence. Her left hand ran through her dust-covered hair. She shook her head. "I mean, how could you leave me to face these..." She stopped. "Did you see what these creatures looked like? And they had me in a cage. And you weren't here. Again."

"Amira," I interrupted her. There was too much angst and anger thrown my way for me to think clearly.

"What happens now?" a female voice piped up behind me.

"Where're we going?"

"Where will you take us?"

"Shouldn't we get going?"

"Who are they?"

Question after question was thrown at me. Pure frustration made me shake my own head.

It was getting too much for me. Any minute now, my own head might explode, the way one of the Xathi's heads had exploded like an overripe marzig melon when it had been hit by one of the blasters.

"I can't...you...don't..." I stumbled over my own words again. Holy dusty spider crap. "Amira. You come with me, Amira."

How the heck was I going to get through this?

"No way. Why should I?" Her stance told me this was not going to be easy.

Briefly, I took my eyes off my sister to let them travel over the sea of people who were looking to me for answers.

How many were there? Fifteen? Twenty? Maybe even thirty? It was too hard to tell. It didn't really matter, either. There were too many for me to deal with.

But there was no choice. The language implants hadn't gathered enough information for Vrehx's men to communicate with the survivors.

Which left me.

"Amira," I turned my attention back to my sister. I just wanted to hold her, to help her deal with her feelings, and to calm her down. "Be reasonable. We need to leave."

"Don't come near me." Her voice rose a little, and her body started to shake. "You're just going to dump me somewhere else. Just like last time. The way you always do. You're always running away, Jeneva. Well, news flash, I'm not running with you."

Shock was setting in.

"Everything alright here?"

I hadn't heard Vrehx come up behind me, his words too soft for the other humans to hear. Tears had started to well up. I had no idea what to do. And yet there was no way I wanted the Skotan to know about my internal struggle and the fight I was having with my sister.

"Yep," I replied as I pressed my lips together.

"Are you taking us?" someone shouted, and I couldn't see who it was.

Vrehx stepped away to speak to his men as one of the human women practically threw herself at him.

"You've got to take us. What if they come back? They killed my father. Please," she started to sob and collapsed at his feet.

"Tu'ver," Vrehx turned away from the woman, spoke quietly. "We will take them all. Get the shuttles ready."

A wave of emotion crossed Tu'ver's face as they moved away from the crowd.

"There'll be trackers, you realize?"

Thunder clouds appeared on the Skotan leader's face.

"I wasn't consulting with you. I was giving you an order."

Tu'ver bowed his head.

"Of course there will be trackers," piped Axtin. "Think of all the fun we're going to have with them later. Let them track us. We'll deal with those miserable srell when we need to."

Tu'ver left the group without another word.

I had nothing to say either.

"Are you coming?" I turned one last time to my sister, too exhausted to meet her glare.

"What if I don't?"

"No one will be here to protect you," I replied quietly. "Looks like everyone else is leaving. You'd better come, too."

Vrehx walked off and I hurried after him. "What about these trackers?" I called out.

He half-turned toward me and waited for me to catch up. "Nothing to worry about, Jeneva. Valorni are a little crazy. They'll have fun."

The lump that had been steadily growing in the back of my throat got even bigger. Fun. There was nothing fun about any of this.

"Ready to head back?" Vrehx continued toward the shuttles.

I turned around one last time to see my sister join the others. Breathing a sigh of relief, I followed Vrehx. At least Amira was safe.

Anything else I could handle later.

VREHX

This was not ideal.

The refugees were reluctant to move or do anything besides grasp each other and look around the shuttle with wide eyes. Understandable, but not helpful.

Thanks to the device implanted in Jeneva, bits and pieces of the human language were now in the computer's database and therefore understandable to me and the rest of the *Vengeance* through our own implants.

However, it was unlikely that these skittish humans would allow themselves to be implanted with translators of their own. I would have to rely on Jeneva in order to understand any unknown words.

I doubted she would enjoy that task.

Now that she was surrounded by people, I noticed

the same distress markers on her face as I did back in the cave where I found her, except now they were amplified.

It was possible she had acutely sensitive hearing, yet she hadn't seemed bothered by the many loud goings-on taking place on the *Vengeance*.

Now she guided the survivors off the shuttles, through the short walk to the ravine.

"Not far, and then we'll be safe," she reassured them, but lines of pain crossed her face. My jaw clenched in irritation. Surely they didn't need her to hold their hands the entire trip?

She held her arm gingerly, making sure she didn't accidentally bump it, speaking to the one who must be her sister. Neither looked happy, which perplexed me. The other pair of sisters had astonishingly strong family bonds. It was logical to assume these two would be happy to be reunited, especially after Jeneva's desperation to reach her sibling.

Apparently not.

"We're going to ditch these shuttles somewhere," Axtin announced.

I nodded in agreement. As much as I would have liked a few extra hands guiding the refugees through the ravine and onto the ship, Axtin and Daxion weren't the most soothing individuals. Perhaps it was better that they go now.

"Make sure you drop them as far away as you can from any civilian population," I instructed.

Axtin gave me a hard look. "Do you really think we're that stupid?"

"Do you really want me to answer that?"

He was silent for a moment before throwing his head back and laughing heartily.

"You're a srell, you know that?" He clapped me on the shoulder.

I felt myself go stiff. Camaraderie during tension was never my forte. Camaraderie in general really wasn't, to be honest.

"No, I'm just smart." Before he could respond, I finished giving orders. "Rig the shuttles with something that will damage the Xathi when they go to retrieve them."

"I can come up with some kind of motion-activated shrapnel bomb," Axtin suggested. "There's a chance it would be ineffective, but if we're damn lucky, it will hit some of them right in their joints."

"Good," I said with a small affirmative nod. "Move out."

Axtin nodded in kind, and left with Dax in tow.

"Tu'ver," I called to the K'ver as he approached. "Find a space suitable for the refugees, and locate any basic supplies we can spare."

"I am going to the med bay to observe Mariella's

healing process," he said, hardly breaking his stride as he entered the ravine. I blinked in surprise.

Strange.

I elected not to dwell on that now. Someone had to handle the refugees.

With Jeneva's coaxing, they followed us through the short passage, until, just like she had, they balked at the ship doors.

"What is this?" an older man demanded suspiciously.

She tangled her hand in her short hair, a snarl twisting her full lips. "Safety. Follow or not, I don't care anymore." Striking as quickly as one of the creatures from her own forest, Jeneva gripped her sister's wrist and dragged her behind as she boarded the *Vengeance*.

With mutters and murmurs, the rest followed. The suspicious man hung back until the end, until a rustle of the moving vines at the mouth of the ravine spurred him to follow.

Finally.

Once inside the safety of the ship, habit took over.

I deactivated my disguise.

So did the rest of my team.

Srell.

The humans gasped and recoiled. Eyes even wider now, they huddled in a mass, lurching from one side of the chamber to another.

Some screamed. Others moved forward with a frantic gleam in their eyes, summoning the courage for a fight.

"What's going on?"

"It's a trap!"

"They're going to kill us!"

Chaos descended as the panicked refugees desperately tried to find a way off the ship.

"Who knew the minds of humans were so fragile," I muttered. "Amazing they haven't died off yet."

"Really?" Jeneva snapped, reaching my side. "You think this was the best way to handle this?"

"It's all right!" She waved her uninjured arm over her head and yelled over the din. "They won't hurt us!"

Only half the humans appeared to be listening to her, but it was enough to slow the crowd's panic.

She lowered her arm, and extended a hand to me as if she meant to touch me, but thought better of it. "They're friends!" It didn't escape my notice that she hesitated just slightly on the last word.

She pressed a hand to the side of her head. Her eyes looked a bit glazed, and she swayed a little on the spot.

"He's brainwashed her!" One of the human males pointed at me. "He's making her say those things to trick us!"

"Oh, for srell's sake," I sighed at the same moment Jeneva yelled, "No, he didn't, dumbass!"

A smile twitched at the corners of my lips. She really could be amusing when she wanted to be.

"Will you tell them they are free to leave if they want to take their chances against the Xathi?" I requested, unwilling to trust my grasp of their language yet.

Jeneva nodded, and relayed my message.

Though I couldn't understand all of what the humans said, they seemed less inclined to riot, if their only other choice was the jungle and the Xathi.

That would do for now. Jeneva bowed her head. I could see the muscles in her jaw working as she clenched her teeth.

"Are you unwell?" I asked stiffly.

"I'm fine," she replied, equally stiff. I was unconvinced. "I have to go talk to my sister." She snaked back through the crowd with less grace than she had before. As I watched her, a sudden realization struck me.

She was an empath. And a terrible one at that. Her blocking skills were basic, at best. I knew of Skotan children who had a better grasp on it than her.

"I'll find a suitable place for these people." Sakev brought my attention back to the situation at hand. "I've just heard from engineering that the weapon didn't come with us through the rift."

"What?" I barked. "How is that even possible?"

"How are we even here?" he shrugged. "But it frees up nearly a quarter of a deck. Plenty of room for them."

"Are you trying to be poetic?" I asked, looking at Sakev from the corner of my eye. "Because if you are, it doesn't suit you." He gave me a srell-eating grin.

"You're just jealous that I have an artistic soul, and you are half a step away from being a cold piece of machinery," he replied. "Do you have a better idea?"

I didn't.

I didn't even know what the humans could do on board. Could they help in anyway? Did we have the food to keep them alive? These uncertainties, the impossible calculations, made my head ache. I had to stop thinking about it. The fact that we had the space was enough for now.

Speaking of headaches, I sought out Jeneva as Sakev urged as many of the humans as he could down a corridor to the innards of the ship. Many were reluctant.

"Go with him," Jeneva urged. I didn't have to be an empath to know her patience was wearing thin. "He's going to take you to where you're going to stay." The other humans nodded in wary understanding.

The sister—Amira, I believe Jeneva called her—refused to move. She grabbed Jeneva by her good arm, forcing Jeneva to focus on her.

"If you think for one second I am going off with

some strange alien, you have another think coming," she snapped.

Jeneva looked tired, the fight I had seen so much of earlier was nearly depleted. The wound on her arm surely wasn't helping.

"Amira," Jeneva tried, but Amira wouldn't let her speak.

"I shouldn't have even been there," she sniffled. "You were the one who moved us there, and then you left! I never wanted to be there."

Amira clearly didn't care if she was overheard or not. She must have assumed that, because she couldn't understand any of us, *we* couldn't understand her.

"I'm sorry," Jeneva said, her voice, barely above a whisper, was strained with emotion. I felt like I was intruding by hearing these private things about Jeneva's life.

"Your sister insisted on coming with us, so she could save your life," I said. I hadn't meant to speak.

Just as I had gone into a blind fury against the Xathi that had injured Jeneva, I had little control. It didn't matter to me that Amira couldn't understand what I said. "I can't imagine why she would take that risk for someone as ungrateful as you. I would consider that before you open your mouth again."

Rage filled Amira's eyes. Clearly, my tone conveyed the message, even if my words were lost on her. I held her gaze, feeling the anger thrumming through my body.

From the corner of my eye, I saw Jeneva shift. She leaned against the wall, resting her head on the cool metal. The bleeding had stopped, but the wound on her arm must have pained her. She should go to med bay... but I had a few things in my cabin that could help. That would be better.

I also suspected the mental strain of her empathic abilities was causing a large portion of her discomfort. Getting her away from her sister would surely help that.

I was about to step closer to her when General Rouhr approached.

"Vrehx," he said.

I nodded in respect.

"Your mission was a success. Though it's unexpected, I support your choice to bring the humans here. We can protect them. Any bloodshed we can prevent is good."

"What is he saying?" Amira's eyes narrowed with suspicion.

The General looked at her, unamused.

"It doesn't concern you," Jeneva answered, her voice breathy and faint. She needed care.

"Don't you tell me what does or doesn't concern me," Amira snapped.

I would handle that in a moment. I turned back to General Rouhr.

"That one's got some fight in her," he said dryly.

"She is Jeneva's sister, sir," I supplied. "It seems to run in the family."

He only nodded. "We will meet in one hour to discuss our options. Go get yourself cleaned up, and take a moment to breathe."

"Thank you, sir," I nodded once more. I returned my attention to Jeneva, who looked pale, and her sister, who didn't seem to care.

"Come with me," I said to Jeneva, cutting off her sister in mid-rant.

"I don't think I can walk very far," Jeneva admitted.

"Not a problem," I said, wrapping one arm around her back and the other behind her knees. I shifted her weight and lifted her off her feet in one swift motion.

"Wait, I -" Jeneva reached out towards her glowering sister.

"You aren't doing anything until that wound is taken care of," I said sternly. I turned my back on Amira, and walked towards my chambers.

JENEVA

I didn't know what to make of Vrehx standing up for me, especially when I agreed with everything Amira said.

I wasn't selfish. I was simply weak. Being around so many people put me on edge, made me feel like my head would explode.

Always had and no matter how hard I tried, I ended up running.

"You're awfully quiet," Vrehx said. "I expected you to put up more of a fight when I picked you up."

"Maybe I'm just more docile than you assumed," I retorted with a smirk, trying to pull my thoughts together.

Something had shifted between us. I wouldn't go as

far as to say I trusted him, but I no longer believed that he was going to kill me the first chance he got.

Actually, he was kind of fun to tease.

"I doubt that," he replied with a small chuckle.

"Was that a laugh I heard?" I asked with mock astonishment. "I didn't think Skotan with massive sticks up their asses could laugh."

"What was that about being more docile?" he asked while looking, literally, down his nose at me.

"Oh, that was bullshit," I said with a casual wave of my hand. "Adrenaline is one hell of a drug, though."

"So are the toxins from a Xathi-inflicted wound," Vrehx said as he rounded the corner.

Oh. Should of thought of that sooner.

Speaking of things I should have thought of... "Where are you taking me?" Everything with the Xathi, with Amira, had thrown me off. The instincts that had kept me alive for over a decade felt dulled by the rapid changes in my life.

"I'm taking you to my cabin so you can rest," he answered. He stopped at a gray door and stood still. A small mechanism burst forward from a compartment in the wall, projecting a grid of thin green lines that criss-crossed Vrehx's face. The mechanism retracted, and the door slid open.

"Your cabin," I repeated slowly. It was more spacious than I'd expected, for being on a ship. The first portion of the room was dedicated to a sleek desk cluttered with maps, star charts, and other documents.

It might have been because I was so out of it, but I swore some of the characters on the pages made sense.

A small step divided the room. Vrehx stepped down into the darker, less cluttered half and placed me on a bed.

His bed.

"You need to brush up on your blocking," he said casually. I tilted my head to look at him. I could feel my confusion written clearly across my face.

"My what? I only had a blaster out there, what was I supposed to block with?" I asked. Now Vrehx looked as confused as I did.

"No, your blocking," he said again, enunciating each syllable as if it would help me understand. "For your empathic abilities." I craned my neck to look at him.

"My *what?*" I asked. "I don't know what you're talking about."

"Is it called something else here?" Vrehx asked, looking genuinely curious. When I only blinked in response, he continued. "The ability to sense the emotions, or even the thoughts, of others."

I felt the color drain from my face.

Vrehx must have seen it, too, for his expression became one of concern. "Is something wrong?"

"No," I said after some consideration. "All my life,

everyone told me what I was feeling wasn't real." A tear slipped down my check. I quickly wiped it away. If I let my control slip now, I don't think I would ever be able to rein it back in. "It was all in my head, my problem."

"We call people with that talent empaths," Vrehx said softly, stroking my hair away from my face.

Empaths. I tested the word in my mind. It felt right.

"How many empaths do you have among your people? Do you know any?" I asked, desperate to learn everything I could.

Vrehx's mouth spread into a full grin. Happy. He actually looked happy.

"All of our women are empaths. It's very useful. Our mating pairs are very strong since the women can feel their mates' feelings." He shook his head and laughed. "There is no safe place to hide for a male who lies to his mate, not that many are foolish enough to try."

"Wow," I said. "Was that two jokes in one day? I fear I've misjudged you."

"Ha! Clever," he deadpanned. But then, his expression softened. "You really don't know how to block?"

"I don't even know what you mean when you say block," I said, looking down at my hands, feeling useless again.

Vrehx reached forward and lifted the wrist of my

injured arm. The bleeding had stopped for the most part, and I hardly felt any pain now.

"When you pick up on another being's emotions, you are actually entering their mind," he explained as he checked my arm. He stood up and strode to a small adjoining room.

"It doesn't feel that way," I replied. "It feels like a thousand hammers banging into my mind. Not the other way around." Vrehx returned with a white square of cloth that smelled like disinfectant.

"This is going to sting a bit," he warned before pressing the cloth to my wound.

I winced and bit down on my bottom lip.

"That's only because your mind is naturally attracted to the minds of others, and you can't control it. Think of it like walking through a doorway in your mind through a doorway into someone else's. To make it stop, all you have to do is shut the door in your mind. That's what blocking is."

"But how do I do that when I can't even find the door?" I asked, frustrated. This was like trying to learn his language without the help of the horrible stabbing ear-bug.

"Let's start by finding my door first," Vrehx suggested. He shifted on the bed, and sat cross-legged directly in front of me. "Face me head on, square your shoulders towards me."

I did as he instructed, feeling more than a little awkward.

"Now, concentrate on reaching out with your mind until you find mine."

I closed my eyes, taking long, deep breaths. This was more than just awkward. It felt like an invasion of privacy on the highest level.

I didn't know where to begin.

I started by picturing his face. His strong jawline, his flaming skin, those fascinating scales. I focused on the energy that radiated from him. Stoic, but with a quiet intensity that I was certain I was feeling now. Yes, yes, I was! I pushed deeper. The sensation of his energy became stronger and stronger until...

"Ow!" I winced as I recoiled both mentally and physically. "What the hell was that?" My head throbbed.

"Essentially, you ran into my door," he said, a smirk on his lips.

"Is your door covered in metal spikes?" I hissed.

"Pretty much," he said. If I didn't know better, I would think there was pride in his voice. *Who am I kidding?* I did know better. There *was* pride in his voice. Smug bastard.

"A well-protected mind is vital," he said, serious once more. "There are some empaths in the world so powerful that they can slip into your mind, and read your very thoughts. They can flip through your memories, they can even change your emotions and you would never even know it happened."

"That's horrible!" I gasped.

"The galaxy is a horrible place," he muttered.

"You can't possibly believe that," I admonished.

He said nothing. Feeling uncomfortable again, I brought the conversation back to mind protection. "So, even if you aren't an empath, you can construct a solid defense?"

"Yes," he said, looking relieved. "Since I can't enter your mind at all, I'll let down my defenses a bit, so you can practice controlling your abilities."

"Are you sure?" I asked. It seemed so...personal.

"Yes," he replied. "Just don't go messing with my head. No telling what you're capable of."

"Very funny," I snipped. I closed my eyes again and found the door guarding his mind. This time, I managed to approach it slowly rather than slamming into it. As I felt his energy with my mind, I detected a small gap.

"Right now," he spoke, nearly breaking my concentration, "I can feel you pressing here." I flinched when I felt his hand lightly touch the side of my temple. "Move around, if you can. Try to understand the way I've constructed the energy in my mind so that you can mimic it."

I did. It was slow progress and my head ached from

the effort. Every time my presence in his mind shifted, he would move his fingers across my forehead or over my hair. Suddenly, he took his hand away and my eyes flew open.

"That was very good," he said with genuine warmth. "We're going to try that again, but this time you are going to point to your location in my head. It's one thing for me to know where I am, but it's another altogether to be able to navigate someone's mind. How else can you expect to find your way back to the door?"

"That can happen?" I asked. "People can get lost in the minds of others?"

"It's rare for my people," he said. "Skotan women are trained to use their abilities at a young age. But, yes, it can happen. Don't worry, I'll snap you out of it if you get lost."

I nodded, taking a deep breath before narrowing in on his mind once more.

I found the door easily. It was open for me, wider than it had been before. I moved my energy through his mind in a slow and controlled manner before collecting it in one place.

"I'm here," I said, letting the tip of my index finger rest above his left eyebrow.

"Close," he said. "You're about an inch to the right. Damn, good job on your first try, though. Try shifting your energy again."

Floating through his mind was surprisingly comfortable. His energy was gentler, softer than I expected it to be. I stopped once more.

"I'm here," I said, reaching for a point near the top of his forehead. I misjudged the distance slightly, causing my fingers to gently trail up his cheek and temple. I felt a flare of warmth ripple through him. A pleasurable sensation traveled from his mind, across the bridge I'd made and into mine.

Suddenly, my energy was being shoved from his mind, his mental door slamming shut.

He stood sharply.

"Too much mental strain at one time can be dangerous," he said quickly, rubbing the back of his neck. "You did a good job, especially for your first time. Rest a bit, then practice strengthening your own door."

"Okay," I said slowly, not knowing what else to say. I wasn't ready to stop. I still had so much more to learn about blocking. To be honest, his energy was nice. I liked his presence.

But it was clear that our lesson was over. And I *was* exhausted, now that he'd mentioned it.

He set a small omni-pad on the nightstand beside the bed. "Use this if you need anything. You can have food brought to you, you can reach me at my station on the bridge, whatever you think you need."

I looked at the device.

"Activate it by pressing your thumb here," Vrehx said, showing me. "Tap here to speak to the internal computer. It's attuned to your voice from your implant and will assist you, although it won't respond back."

Once he saw that I had nodded in understanding, he turned away before I could say anything else.

I wiggled under the covers and rolled over on my side, with my back facing the doorway. I realized I hadn't heard the door slide open and shut. Vrehx hadn't left yet.

"By the way," I called over my shoulder. I was already half asleep. "Thank you for saving my life back there." There was a long beat of silence.

"You're welcome."

VREHX

I needed to pull myself together. *Immediately.*

I didn't understand it. My mother was an empath, my sister had nearly completed her own training. They'd both entered my mind frequently, but it had never felt like *that*.

For a human who'd lived her entire life not knowing about her abilities, Jeneva was incredibly powerful. With the right training, she could rival the best Skotan empaths.

But, that heat, that desire, had shot through me like a bolt of electricity…I couldn't even say for certain whether it came from me or from her.

That was dangerous. Jeneva was dangerous.

Even now, I was thinking about her when I needed

to be thinking about the Xathi, the war, and the rift; not to mention the refugees I'd brought onboard.

This whole situation was messy enough. I couldn't allow Jeneva to complicate it any further.

I spotted Tu'ver as I made my way to the bridge. It looked like he was leaving the med bay. He nodded when he saw me, and fell into step beside me.

"How is the other human's recovery progressing?" I asked, more to be polite than anything else. The longer we were stuck on this planet, the more I realized we would have to completely rely on each other. I'd seen friendships save lives in combat.

I might never consider Tu'ver, Axtin, or any of the others friends, but I would like to think that, given the choice between helping me or letting me fall, they would help.

"Mariella," Tu'ver said, his tone level. "Her name is Mariella. She's progressing well. She should be up and about soon."

"That's good to hear," I said, even though I found it quite difficult to actually care about the human female. Jeneva was interesting because, well, she was Jeneva.

I tried to make conversation, but neither of us were particularly good at small talk. We parted ways without a word when we reached the bridge. I didn't know where he was going, I didn't think to ask.

General Rouhr, Sk'lar, and Karzin were already in

the com room, waiting. No one had taken a seat at the oblong table, each preferring to stand or lean. Thribb, the Sugavian engineer, rapidly input something into his omnipad. I had never spoken directly to the engineer, though I had watched him work. He was closer to a computer than an actual flesh and blood being, at least mentally.

"Thank you for gracing us with your presence," Karzin grumbled. In typical Valorni fashion, he was unbelievably impatient.

"I'm sorry, did you have an appointment to smash your head into a boulder?" I snapped. So much for being polite.

"Enough," General Rouhr snarled. He looked as on edge as I felt, which was saying something. It took a lot to ruffle the General. "Vrehx, I said an hour. Was I unclear?"

"No, sir. Apologies," I nodded curtly. I hoped he wouldn't press further. I didn't know how I would explain what I was doing with Jeneva.

Even simply thinking about her brought on a rush of that same heat I'd felt when her mind had touched mine. I had to snap myself out of it.

"Fine. We were just going over the sparse intel we'd been able to gather thus far," General Rouhr continued, to my relief.

I was grateful to have something important to focus

on. Information that could be implemented and controlled. Control would be welcome.

"We'd been producing neuro translators since the refugees came aboard," Karzin said. "Soon, we'll have enough for all of them. The real issue will be getting them to agree to it."

"One of the humans who has already been given the implant would be best to assist with that," General Rouhr replied. He turned to me. "Ask Jeneva to do it. I like her. She's direct, she gets things done."

"She also doesn't follow orders well," I argued. "And other than her sister, I do not believe she has any relationship with the other refugees. They may not grant her any authority."

I didn't like the idea of her exposed to that crowd. Not until she'd perfected her blocking. They weren't worth the risk.

"I don't think we should be pouring resources into the refugees at all," Sk'lar cut in, to my relief. "Those transmitters are taxing to produce and we don't know how long any of our stores will hold out. We have to focus on conserving."

"If we implant the refugees, it is more likely they can help us locate more resources to help us replenish our stores," Karzin replied as if he were talking to a child.

"If this planet has resources we *can* use," Sk'lar argued.

"That's something I'm working on as we speak," Thribb, the engineer, interjected suddenly. I realized this was the first time I'd ever heard him speak. He didn't look up from his omnipad. "I'm starting up a broad-spectrum scan of the planet for compatible resources, or at least, attempting to."

"What's the difficulty?" I asked.

"Ordinarily," Thribb began, still not looking up, "I could utilize our satellites to quickly sweep large areas at a time. From there, I could deploy a probe. Resources could be collected in as little as a day."

"Yes, I'm aware," I said, my patience wearing thin. Thribb did not acknowledge that I'd spoken.

"The problem is the rift," he continued. "It interferes with the signals. I have to use the ship's sensors to locate potential resources. It's time consuming and imprecise, not to mention the toll it takes on our power supplies."

"Exactly," Sk'lar interjected. "The sensors were already working overtime, so we shouldn't waste power fabricating tech that the humans will likely reject in the first place."

"But if the humans could help us locate resources faster than the scanner, which seems likely, they need to be implanted as soon as possible," Karzin argued, and they snarled, going around the circular argument yet again.

"As of right now," Thribb interjected, "I am only scanning for basic resources. If that goes well, I'll know the ship's scanner can handle finding something much more complex. But, like I said, it's a process."

"You said that the rift is interfering with satellite signals," I repeated. "It takes a considerable amount of energy to disrupt our equipment like that. Is there any way we can harness the energy from the rift itself?"

"If the rift was a stable energy source, then, yes," Thribb said before falling silent once more.

"But..." I prompted, trying not to roll my eyes nor give off any other physical indication of my frustration. At least the conversation was steering away from the humans. It was almost a physical effort not to think about Jeneva.

"The rift is literally a tear in the fabric of space and time," Thribb continued. "It's impossible to say that what's on the other side is the exact place where we fell through. It's constantly shifting and remolding itself, for reasons I can't measure from here."

"That would explain why more Xathi haven't come through," General Rouhr mused before nodding to Thribb to continue.

"Exactly. I sent two satellites up to investigate the rift immediately after we crashed. One couldn't even get to the rift. The energy waves all but tore it to shreds. The other did manage to pass through the rift, only to disappear as soon as it passed through to the other side. A fluke. We can't throw more resources at it, hoping to replicate it."

"Was that just a really long way of saying we can't go through the rift, even if we could break from the gravity well?" Karzin asked, scowling.

I silently agreed with his sentiments, but the engineer couldn't be hurried. And on this side of the rift, he was all we had.

"That was a really long way of saying we don't even know what's on the other side," Thribb said with a wry smile. "As far as harnessing its energy, it's simply too unpredictable. Even if our tech could interact with the rift without getting fried, there's nothing to safeguard the *Vengeance* against a complete overload."

"And that was just a long way of saying what exactly?" Karzin snapped, becoming increasingly frustrated. I hid my smirk.

"Too much energy make spaceship blow up," Thribb replied.

Karzin growled.

"So," I said quickly, trying to restore order. "We can't use the rift's energy and we can't travel back through the rift to get home. What is our top priority?"

"I would think, finding a way to power the ship," Thribb said.

"Right," I continued. "So, the less power we use from

our stores, the better. Karzin, how many neural transmitters have been produced so far?"

"We can implant about half the refugees," he answered.

"Okay, good. Stop production for now, and we'll fit the most useful humans with the neural transmitters. Sound fair?"

Karzin nodded.

Good, this was progress. This was order.

"There's still the issue of what we are going to *do* with all the humans," Sk'lar interjected.

"We'll tackle that once we have them fitted with the transmitters," I said. "Jeneva can't be the only one with experience with the local flora. Fauna. Whatever those things are. Once the humans are implanted, they can assist in procuring basic resources. Food, water, anything that won't kill us on this hellhole of a planet. Thribb, start scanning for those." Thribb nodded and punched something into the omnipad, while I thought about the next steps. "Ideally, what would you need to ensure the *Vengeance* doesn't completely lose power?"

"It is unlikely that the exact fuels the *Vengeance* is designed to use will be found on this planet. However, I may be able to find something we can convert with minimal effort." He flicked to a new screen, filled with more gibberish. "I did a preliminary, non-specific scan of the area while I was investigating the rift."

"Thribb, please, small sentences," I said with a wince. The barrage of information combined with Thribb's grating voice was giving me a headache. Maybe not having him speak was for the best.

"I can compile a list of alternative materials," he said, once again unfazed by my harshness.

"Fantastic. When can you have the list?" I asked. Thribb resumed his rapid taps into the omnipad.

"Approximately seven minutes and forty-three seconds."

"Great. We'll wait for you," I said. Thribb quickly exited the bridge.

As soon as the doors slid closed once more, Karzin sighed. "Srell, we could have powered up the *Vengeance* with a hand crank in the time it took him to finish a thought."

"Brilliant minds are not always palatable to all," General Rouhr said in a warning tone.

"No disrespect intended, sir," Karzin shrugged.

General Rouhr held his gaze until the Valorni dropped his eyes, then turned to me.

"You handled that well."

"Thank you, sir." But my mind wasn't on the compliment.

We all remained silent as we waited for Thribb to return.

For seven minutes, all I could think about was that we might never be able to go home again.

I'd been too busy for the reality to sink in. But here we were, and unless physics had a surprise for us, here we'd stay.

It was a long seven minutes.

JENEVA

In the dim light of the sleeping quarters, it all came flooding back to me. Arguing with my sister, Vrehx carrying me to his cabin, learning I was an empath…the relief I felt was overwhelming. My whole life, I had let myself be convinced that there was something wrong with me, that I'd never be able to live a normal life. It turned out, I just had an enhanced ability. One that could be controlled.

Stretching in the soft bedding, I replayed the touch of Vrehx's mind. It hadn't been harsh and cold like I'd expected.

Had I imagined that quick jolt of pleasure that shot through him when I touched him? Or had that been my own response?

Pushing unanswerable questions away, I sat up in

bed, closed my eyes, and tried to narrow my focus. I pictured a doorway opening and closing.

He'd told me to practice building my mental shield, mastering that doorway between my mind and someone else's. If I could master this empathic gift, I could return to town. I could finally be there for my sister.

I visualized blocking everyone else's thoughts from my brain. Ten minutes went by. I didn't feel anything like what I'd felt when I was working with Vrehx. Maybe it was due to the fact I didn't have another mind to interact with.

Getting to my feet, I noticed that much of the pain had faded from where the Xathi clipped me. The muscles were still somewhat sore, but it was a large improvement. I took a moment to smooth out the covers of Vrehx's bed, wanting to be a polite guest, before leaving his cabin.

Once in the hallway, I realized I had no idea where I was. Uncertainty tightened my throat. I didn't think Vrehx was a threat, but that didn't mean I wanted to be caught unawares by any of the other crew members.

I felt my sister's emotions almost immediately. Angry and tense, like a caged animal. I followed her volatile energy through the steel labyrinth of the *Vengeance's* corridors. As I walked, I practiced building mental shields and taking them down. I couldn't completely drown out the emotions of those around me, but I could dim them. It was enough for me for the moment.

I approached a large door. From the intensity and the sheer number of the emotions I sensed, I knew this was where the refugees were being kept. Only the fact that I finally knew what it was I was experiencing kept it from being overwhelming.

The door to the room was completely open, yet guarded by two aliens. Two Valorni, if what I had picked up on by listening to crew chatter was correct.

"Why are you guarding the refugees?" I asked, noting the massive guns each Valorni was carrying.

"I wouldn't put it past them not to riot," one replied. He was big, more than a foot taller than me. He sounded almost eager for the refugees to try something. I suppressed a shudder, and walked through the open doorway.

I spotted Amira instantly, kneeling beside a man who looked like he had a considerable injury in his side. Her brow was furrowed in worry as she spoke to the person examining the wound. She kept tucking and re-tucking her long hair behind her ear, a nervous habit she'd had since she was young. Her eyes snapped to mine as if she sensed my presence.

She was on her feet in one smooth motion. Her

anger swelled and slammed into me, but behind it there was a trace of something else... fear, worry.

I could understand that. She'd never been in control of her own life, and now things must seem to be spiraling away from her.

Taking a deep breath, I fought to strengthen my shield, to close that door between my mind and hers, but it was like trying to keep out a flash flood.

"What do you want?" she snapped.

"Is that a friend?" I asked, looking to the man she had been kneeling in front of before.

"That's none of your business," she replied. My heart ached. I took after our father in looks and temperament. But she was our mother made over.

"I came down here to check on you," I said, fighting to keep my voice level.

"Now you're coming to check up on me?" Amira asked, her voice rising, her ever present anger spilling over.

"I came as soon as I could," I said weakly. My head ached. I felt ill, but not entirely from the strain on my abilities.

"It wasn't enough," Amira hissed. "Nothing you've done since mom and dad died has ever been enough."

Her anger was too much. My vision blurred. I was going to collapse if I didn't put some distance between us. Every muscle in my body was weary. Maybe someday I could be the sister she needed, but right now I couldn't.

"I can't do this," I whispered, walking slowly backwards towards the doorway I had just come through.

Amira paused, a flicker of regret on her face, then turned her back on me and rejoined the huddled survivors.

I hurried back through the corridor, wiping my tears off my cheeks as I walked blindly through the hallways, anxious to get away from Amira's intensity. The more distance I put between me and her, the abler I was to construct a mental shield.

Then something familiar brushed against my mind. Vrehx's energy at the edges of my mental shield. He was warm, steady. I lowered my shield again, opening the door between us.

My idea was to let him know I was nearby, that I was practicing like he told me to.

Instead, fragments of conversation drifted through. I started to slam the door shut, cheeks flaming at the invasion of privacy, but one phrase caught me, held me fast despite my best intentions.

"What is the plan with regards to the refugees?" It was a voice I hadn't heard before, but if they were discussing the refugees, that meant Amira. Which meant I needed to know what was going on.

"We're going to protect them, Sk'lar," another said. "No matter how hard you argue against it." I vaguely recognized that voice, but I couldn't put a name to it.

"I still don't think we have the resources for that. We don't know how long we're going to be stuck here. We don't know if we'll be able to relocate them. There are a lot of variables that can't be calculated," Sk'lar replied. "Besides, the *Vengeance* isn't meant to be grounded. It's putting strain on the hull, systems are out of sync, it's like the ship herself is throwing a tantrum."

"All the more reason to accommodate the refugees." I certainly recognized the voice of General Rouhr. "They may have information that could help us get us out of the gravity well. Of course, there is still the problem of conserving power. Thribb, give us an engineer's perspective."

"Without the engines fully online, we are drawing exclusively from ship's reserves," someone with an odd grating voice answered, presumably Thribb. "Before long, we will be unable to use the cloaking device, the food replicator, or the waste systems. The med bay won't be able to function properly. Our computers and scanners will be useless."

"What do we need to stop that from happening?" It was Vrehx. I could feel the burning intensity inside him.

"Nadrium," Thribb's reply. "A rare mineral with an

unusual molecular structure. It's incredibly versatile, and a small amount goes a long way. The onboard computer scanners are searching for potential nadrium deposits, but it's slow going without satellites. And even if we get hold of enough, we don't have the equipment to refine it."

"Perhaps that is something else the natives can assist with," General Rouhr said thoughtfully.

"That would be ideal," Thribb agreed.

The discussion continued, but I had heard enough. The situation was simple. The ship needs something to power it. *No power, no survival.* Nadrium equals power.

Survival was my specialty. It was about time I put that skill to use.

I found my way to the bridge. Thankfully, the crew members paid me no mind as I hurried to an open computer terminal in the corner of the room. I was planning to wander blindly through the database, hoping there would be pictures to help me understand what I was looking at. But, to my surprise, I could understand the majority of the characters on the screen. Was this the work of the neural device in my ear? Vrehx hadn't mentioned anything about affecting my ability to *read* another language. But I'd recognized some of the writing on the papers on his desk. At this point, after everything that had happened, I wasn't in the position to question anything.

I searched through the interface until I found the program running the search for nadrium.

The computer was doing a broad search of the entire world. At the rate it was going, it could take months to narrow in on a specific mineral deposit.

There had to be a smarter way to see if it was even on this planet. I tapped my fingers on the edge of the console. The town of Einhiv mined materials for power units in all of the colony towns. I wasn't sure if they used nadrium, though. I'd lived without power for years, and for all I knew, it could be the same mineral with a different name.

An icon at the copy of the screen looked like two squares, one slightly covering the other. Maybe...

Yes! Tapping that made a duplicate of the search. A sketchy map showed enough of the area that I could narrow it down to the radius around Einhiv.

The flashing button looked like it meant to run the program. One press, and something was happening.

Hopefully I hadn't done anything terrible. Waiting for the results, I glanced around the bridge.

A few of the men gave me curious looks, but no one seemed upset by what I was doing.

That was good, right?

A soft ding called my attention back to the screen. I scrolled through the list of minerals that had been detected in the region of Einhiv, muttering a quiet prayer.

At the very bottom of the list was an almost undetectable amount of nadrium, but it was giving off a disproportionately large power signature.

"I can't believe it worked," I mumbled to myself. I was always good at this sort of thing in school. I liked working with computers because they didn't give me migraines the way people did. Nice to have it finally be useful.

A niggling thought struck me. The engineer, Thribb, had mentioned something about a lack of refining equipment.

Just finding the nadrium wasn't enough.

I dug into the computer's files one more time to see if I could ascertain the state the mineral needed to be in so that it could power the ship.

I ended up rifling through the schematics for the power units of the *Vengeance*. I hoped no one had taken notice of what I was doing. From an outsider's perspective, it probably looked like sabotage.

I located the parameters for refined nadrium and plugged them into the search program, limiting the initial search to all the larger towns.

If we were going to do this, it needed to be fast. Something on the other side of the continent wasn't going to help.

As the computer worked its magic, I tried to reach out to Vrehx's mind. He had to know about this, tell the others. I felt a faint tingle against my consciousness, but nothing more. I'd have to practice more.

Another ding, and all other thoughts were swept away.

In the entire area, there was only one potential source.

Duvest, the original landing site of the colony ship.

Hell.

VREHX

I tried to pay attention to my strike team as we ate. They went on and on about the planet, the people, the wild forest, the creatures.

My mind wandered back to Jeneva with every topic.

"Hey, Vrehx, what do you think?" Axtin piped up.

I had no idea what he was talking about. I sat there, blinking at him. Axtin shrugged, and they carried on with their conversation.

I caught a snippet, though. Now they were discussing the ship's food quality. I was glad I'd missed it.

The food was terrible and everybody knew it.

Why keep talking about it?

I abruptly got up and walked away, bored. The mess

hall was sterile and uninviting, and I wasn't hungry anyway.

There was only one person I wanted to speak to.

I went to my quarters to find Jeneva, but she wasn't there.

Where the srell is she?

I turned down another corridor. They all looked the same, only years serving on various ships kept me from being disoriented.

My brain conjured an image of her wandering aimlessly. There were computers and other crewmen to ask for directions, but what if she didn't know that? What if they frightened her?

I pictured a small and helpless creature, lost and vulnerable to danger.

A small part of my mind laughed at that, but I couldn't let the image go.

She couldn't have gone far. I lowered the barricade in my mind and sought her out. A wave of despair, anger, and a glimmer of hope hit me.

Something was wrong.

I blinked back the initial shock and sped down the corridor.

What was she doing on the bridge?

The tightness in my chest eased as I saw her at a spare terminal in the far corner. Her jacket hung over the seat, and the skintight sleeveless work shirt revealed her shape.

Not the hard muscles and sharp angles of my people. She was soft, her gentle curves shifting with every breath she took.

Different.

Alluring.

A quiet snort came from Karzin's station, but I ignored him to find out what had caused such a mix of emotions from Jeneva.

She sat in front of the monitor with a look of total concentration on her face, as if she were born to operate the systems. I could tell she knew I was there, but she didn't acknowledge me until I stood directly behind her.

"Look at this," she said without turning around. "I think it's what we need to get moving."

I leaned down and looked over her shoulder to see what she had found and blinked.

It was a map showing the nadrium signature. That was the hope I felt from her.

Her emotions seemed a little backwards. If I had discovered something like that, I would be overjoyed. What was the problem?

Always a mystery with her. Her mind was still open to mine, tempting me to take a quick peek.

The sister again. I should have known. Jeneva

grieved for a lost connection with the only family she had left. And she blamed herself for it.

Ridiculous, but the issue would have to wait.

I peered over her shoulder to study the location of the signature. Not far. Even allowing for extra time to fight off the charming creatures of this planet, I could have some back to Thribb long before our stores had the slightest dent in them.

Finally, a positive surprise.

"I'll assemble the strike team, head out immediately." I squeezed her shoulder lightly, relishing her smooth skin under my fingers. "Good thinking."

Instead of going, though, I stayed where I was.

Her breathing had tightened at my touch, and I could see the curve of her breasts peeking above the neckline of her shirt, nipples tightening into hard buds, pushing against the forest green fabric.

My cock swelled, and I had to force back the urge to brush my hand over the soft cushions, roll the nubs between my fingers until she groaned my name.

I stood abruptly and turned to go back to the mess hall. I could have called my team to the bridge, but I needed to put some distance between Jeneva and me for a while.

She pulled the jacket back on and followed me to the corridor, ruining my escape.

"The strike team? Are you nuts?"

"What do nuts have to do with it?"

"Mentally insane. Are you fucking mentally insane?" She smacked me lightly on the arm.

Oh. A human metaphor. My first one, and I already hated them all.

"How else do you think we're going to acquire the nadrium if no one goes?"

"I know this town, Duvest. I'll go."

"You want to leave the safety of the ship." It was half a question and half an incredulous realization.

She craned her neck to look me in the eye. "Yes."

"No. Forget it." I stopped, looked down on her to assert my authority.

The fire in her eyes told me she was having none of it. She lifted her chin. "Do *you* have a better idea?" she challenged.

"I'll go with my team." I repeated, frustrated. "You'll stay here."

"Forget it. Even with the disguises, you think they're just going to hand that shit over to strangers? Hell, no. I'm going."

"You're a civilian under our protection." My voice dropped, became a husky growl. "Under my protection."

Did she realize she had just closed the gap between us by a few centimeters?

Jeneva stared at me defiantly, but her pupils were dilated, her chest heaved, ragged breaths stirring me.

This thing, this madness between us. She felt it, too.

Lip raised in almost a snarl, she stepped closer, forcing me to bite back my own groan as her soft breasts brushed against my chest.

"Am I under your protection, or your prisoner?" The tip of her pink tongue peeked out, fixing my attention on her full lips."You can't stop me. I'm going."

I opened my mouth to argue; instead I grabbed the back of her head, tangling my fingers in her short hair, while my free arm snaked around her waist.

I pulled her tightly against me, the crush of our bodies against each other burning despite the layers of fabric.

Her eyes widened just a fraction and I waited to see if she would resist, stiffen, pull away.

I'd let her go. I would make myself let her go.

Instead, she poured fuel on the fire, sliding her hands up my chest and around my neck, tilting her face up to meet me.

I fell upon her mouth, nipping and sipping at her lips until she opened, welcoming me. I drove my tongue in, winding it around hers.

The taste of her, the scent of her, filled my senses, only increased my burning need to touch more of her silken skin.

My cock pulsed, hard against her, and she let out a little whimper, pressing herself closer against me.

I broke off, forehead pressed to hers while I gathered my thoughts.

"We have to stop," I whispered, breath having left me.

Her eyes blinked in confusion, the lust-filled haze echoing my own. "What? Why?" she panted.

I laced my fingers through hers, unwilling to deprive myself of all touch, knowing that anything further would be a mistake.

"Because unless you want me to bend you over and claim you in the middle of the corridor, we need to get back to my quarters."

She stumbled at my words. "Oh."

Through my block, I could feel her spike of arousal at my words, heightening my own. The image of her bared to me, pushed against the corridor wall, every hidden fold exposed to me, filled my mind. I couldn't tell if it was my imagination or hers.

It didn't matter.

Fuck it, I growled, spinning to lift her into my arms. The hell with what anyone else thought.

If carrying her led to ship's gossip, acting on the growing urge to play out the scene in my mind would only be worse.

After an eternity, my cabin door opened. The bed

lay only a few steps away, but now that we were in the privacy of my quarters, I couldn't wait. I knocked the desk clean with one sweep, setting her down on the edge of the table.

"Last chance to tell me to stop," I managed. My hands flexed at my sides. I would stop. I could stop. "This is probably a terrible idea."

With one smooth motion, she slid the jacket off her arms and leaned forwards, her hands slowly tracing their way up my chest to wrap around my shoulders, then they slid down until her tiny, fragile fingers traced patterns on my hands.

"I'm not planning on stopping," she breathed. "What you do is up to you, of course." The teasing twinkle in her eye released the tight band at my chest. I stepped forward between her knees and slowly, reverently, drew the tank top off her body.

Her soft breasts seemed to beg for my tongue.

She pulled away slightly. "I know they're not particularly big." For a second, I felt shame leaking around the gaps in her block.

"They're perfect," I growled. "Everything is perfect." As I wrapped one hand around her back, the other explored those alluring curves, stroking, kneading, until she arched in my hands.

Slowly, I eased her back until she lay on the table before me, chest heaving at the attention.

. . .

I SET my mouth on her nipple and flicked it with my tongue. She gasped and arched her back, moving her hips against me.

I moved to the other nipple, sucking and tugging. She moaned and quivered underneath me. I traced my tongue between her breasts and down her stomach, tasting her strange softness. With a flash of clarity, I knew that no matter how much of her I covered, I would always crave more.

She shivered and rested her hand on my head, fingers trailing my scales, brushing the curve of my ears, the cords of my neck.

More. I had to have more.

My fingers grazed the waistband of her pants. An unspoken question that she answered with slight roll of her hips. I unfastened the closure carefully, each inch of exposed skin shredding my nerves until my hands almost shook with anticipation.

"Vrehx," she growled out in frustration, shimmying her hips under my hands, wiggling until, with one quick push, her pants and undergarment were at her knees. "If you mean it," she panted, "stop teasing."

Demanding little mate. I chuckled, then knelt between her legs to draw off her boots and finish pulling her pants down. I trailed kisses up her ankle to her knee, licking and nipping my way towards her core.

Damn. I should have checked the other human female's med bay records, made sure we were compatible.

Resolve was steeled by her delicate scent.

We would have to be. Surely this madness could only be resolved one way.

At the top of her thighs, I pulled both her knees onto my shoulders, rocking forward to examine the tender pink slit before me.

Tenderly, I ran my finger up her seam, listening as she hissed at my touch.

"You'll have to tell me when something's wrong," I ground out. A tiny nub sat at the top of the slit. I circled it lightly and she shuddered.

"You're doing fine," she panted.

I stroked her again, ending each touch with a caress of the tender nub, until her wetness coated my fingers. The scent tempted me until I licked once, her cry of pleasure making my cock even harder.

"Delicious," I growled. My tongue replaced my fingers, and she curled from the table. I reached forward with both arms wrapped around her legs, holding her still, pinned and open.

At the flick of my tongue through the opening of

her slit, Jeneva twitched, her inner muscles contracting around me.

Encouraged, I alternated penetrating her with my tongue and slow sucks of the nub, driven faster by her cries, the taste of her warmth. Until, with one shattering cry, she spasmed, writhing on the table.

"Vrexh," she screamed once, then with a final spasm, she lay still, panting.

Srell.

I'd hurt her.

JENEVA

That was…

I shook my head, reality stealing back in. I didn't even have the words for what that was. Half the time, I thought I hated Vrehx. He was arrogant, pushy, a know-it-all.

I'd never really thought I had a 'type', but he wouldn't have been it.

Even if he'd been human.

Apparently my body had other plans. He wasn't a bad guy, and when we touched, when my mind opened to his, well…

That certainly wasn't hate.

Gently he lifted me from the desk, carried me to his bed until we settled, me still nestled in his arms.

"Are you all right?" Those strange red eyes looked concerned, almost worried.

A shaky laugh was the best I could manage as I snuggled into his embrace. Just for a few more minutes, then I'd get back to reality.

"More than all right, silly."

Vrehx laid me against the pillows and slipped out to the small side room, coming back with a wet cloth and slowly began to clean me. Each swipe of the cloth sent aftershocks through my core as I lay, still breathless.

"I think you are the only person to have ever called me silly," he commented mildly.

I reached for him, pulled him back down to lie next to me. He idly brushed the side of my breast and I gasped, pressed into him. I might not completely know what I was doing here, but my body obviously wanted more from him.

"You seem a little overdressed for the occasion." I swept my hand down his uniform. Then a thought struck. "Unless...do your people have prohibitions about nudity?"

Oh my God. This wasn't good. I had jerked my shirt off, desperate for his touch, without even thinking about all the ways we were different.

And then my mind froze. All the ways.

Could we even, would...

How would this even work?

Vrehx laughed. "Of all the things we have rules about, nudity is not one of them." He undid the fastening of that tight uniform shirt and shocked me by letting it fall to the floor. "I simply had other matters on my mind."

The heat in his smile coiled through my belly, then suddenly he frowned. "Are you sure you're not injured? Your reaction seemed extreme."

Extreme. Well, that's one way of putting it.

I flushed. "I haven't exactly had that strong of a reaction before."

His frown deepened and I laid my hand across the hard planes of his chest to reassure him.

"But that meant what you were doing felt very, very good."

He smoothed down the skin of my rib cage, over the curve of my hip, then back up. "So the louder you react, the more pleasurable the experience is for you?"

I paused, considering. This would be a good conversation to not screw up.

"That's about right. It's not always so simple, but I promise I'll tell you if I need you to stop."

"In that case," he grinned, pulled me tighter to him, and traced one finger over my clit, "I can't wait to hear you again."

He slid one finger between my slick nether lips and joined it with a second, pumping in and out slowly.

I squirmed until I faced him. "If we're playing that game, then I think this is only fair." I reached for the stiff bulge at the front of his pants, grasping him through the taut fabric. Stroking the hard length of him, my mind whirled. I hadn't seen him yet, but just by touch he was wide, and long. And definitely not shaped how I'd expected.

He pulled my hand away, pinning my wrists above my head with one hand while the other resumed its place between my thighs.

"Later," he murmured, then locked my lips with his own, thrusting his tongue into my mouth in time with the penetration of his fingers at my core, driving and grinding into me until, helpless against the assault on my senses, I shattered, screaming his name again.

Still, he wrung the last quivering drops of pleasure from me until I lay, spent and exhausted beside him.

As the last shivers worked through me, my mind whirled. What had I done?

What did I even know about this man, these people?

I pulled away slightly, making sure my mental door was locked, bolted tight.

"Jeneva," Vrehx murmured, one hand cradling my shoulder.

I shrugged him off, rolled away.

I had to pull it together.

Whatever he thought, he and his band of merry men weren't going to be able to get into Duvest.

And this, my mind stuttered, thinking about how it felt when he touched me, when I gave in to the demands of his questing hands…

Whatever this was. It wasn't getting me any closer to my goal.

I might not know what this was, but I knew how to survive.

Priorities.

Without a word, I slipped from the bed, gathered my clothes, and redressed.

Vrehx said nothing, just watched me from the bed, eyes grown cold, face blank.

Fine. It was easier if he was being an asshole.

I paused at the door, just for a moment. If he'd asked me where I was going, I would've told him.

Probably.

As it was, he didn't ask. He didn't say anything.

His lack of words felt like a slap in the face.

As the door closed behind me, I took a deep breath, then I started to run. I needed to get the nadrium to protect my sister and get this alien craft operating so it could save everyone on board and on the planet.

Time to show these aliens what a human female could do.

VREHX

Well.
    We just shared ourselves with one another.

Shared something soul-shattering.

And she just snuck out of the room.

She's annoying, stubborn, thick-headed, and a massive pain in my scaly ass.

How could I have allowed myself to feel *anything* for her?

And here I was, letting this…this…*human* woman seduce me, vex me, and pleasure me. How could I have let her get to me like this? What was it about Jeneva that made me lose control of my senses?

I put my arms under my head and took a deep breath. Deep breath in, count to six, then, slowly, deep breath out. It was one of the things my father had taught me to regain control of my senses.

"You need to control your breathing if you're to think clearly and quickly, my son. A warrior loses his fight if he allows emotions and panic to control him. Always breathe deep, always think clearly. Use your emotions for yourself. Never let your emotions use you."

My father would begin and end every lesson with those words. It was his way of regaining control of himself, of getting *me* to control myself.

I had to breathe… It was the one thing I always tried to remember.

I took a deep breath and thought about what Jeneva would try to do. Our conversation, before we stopped talking, before we'd been lost in each other's bodies, had been about the nadrium and where we could find it.

Oh, by all that creates order, she's going to go after the nadrium. She's going to try to get it on her own. Oh, what a pain this female is.

As a snarl escaped my lips, I jumped out of bed and got dressed. Damn that infernal woman! She's going to get herself killed out there.

I jammed my feet into my boots, swung my belt around my waist, and rushed out of my room. First things first, we needed supplies. The armory was two

decks down from my quarters, so I made my way down
the tubes, avoiding the elevators.

I wanted to avoid the others and their snide
remarks, as well.

Regardless of how disrespectful it was to ridicule
your commander, it didn't bother me on a personal
level.

What did bother me was that they were right. I had
let myself be weakened by this human woman.

I lost my temper because of her. I went berserk
because of her. I lost control because of this woman—
and that was not something I could accept about
myself.

As I made my way down the tubes, sliding down the
ladders, I tried to control my thoughts. What we really
needed was a well thought-out and planned mission to
get the nadrium. This damn planet was more insane
than any other place I had ever been.

The damn plants fight back, and the animals are
nearly as dangerous as the Xathi. Jeneva needed my
protection.

I punched in my code to the armory. The doors
opened, and I was greeted by Axtin's second-favorite
sight on the entire ship. The wall to my left was loaded
with weapons of all sorts—hand blasters, Tu'ver's
sniper rifles, grenades, smoke bombs, neural whips,

knives, long-blades, axes, and mobile self-defense turrets.

On the right wall—armor, space suits with air tanks, packs of different sizes, and Axtin's personal stash of augmentations. The idiot didn't throw anything away.

The far wall in front of me was where the survival gear was hung, along with the ammunition for our blasters. I grabbed two packs, filling one with some cable and several med-kits.

Idiot woman had no armor of her own. Bad design, these humans. Just soft flesh, curves, smooth thighs, supple breasts...

I was forced to shake my head and breathe. Oh, how I hated that woman. She made my mind wander, out of control.

Back to the matter at hand. Three—no, four—med-kits. Humans were fragile. Two lengths of cable, three braces of knives, a stasis box for the nadrium, and some rations spread between the two packs. I took no chances and fitted myself with a new holographic projector, keyed to match my last 'disguise'.

I strapped two blasters on me, one on my left thigh and the other on my right. I put two more blasters in my pack and filled hers with additional ammunition. Putting both packs on, I tested my movement and balance.

I had to rearrange one of the packs a bit, but I finally found a solid balance.

I left the armory and used my code to lock it up. Fifteen minutes spent inside... By all that is holy and orderly, that infernal woman had destroyed my concentration.

She'd been alone for too long, nearly thirty minutes since she left my room, left my bed.

Our bed, a soft voice at the back of my mind insisted.

I shut it down, focused on more important things. She could be anywhere by now. She could already be injured, attacked by the Xathi. Attacked by her own damn planet.

I headed out of the *Vengeance* and tried to open my mind to connect to her.

Damn it. She was blocking me. My pride in her skills was balanced by frustration.

I could feel her, but I wasn't sure what direction she had gone in.

Luckily, her skills at obfuscation were no match for my skills at tracking. It wasn't hard to find her tracks a few hundred yards from the ship.

Why was she going in this direction? The nadrium wasn't this way. Or did she know something I didn't?

Travelling through the forest we had destroyed was an awkward combination of simple and difficult. With the ruined and mangled trees lying on the ground, I was able to see everything around me for hundreds of yards, but there were several times when I had to climb over fallen trees to continue on.

Where in the world was this woman headed?

After an hour of tracking her, I finally saw her ahead of me. I opened my mind to her again, wanting her attention without calling the wrath of the forest down on us. She flung her arms in the air, turned towards me, and yelled at me mentally.

Her mental voice was loud, bringing me pain for the split-second it took me to close our connection again. She waited for me to get within a few feet of her before she tore into me.

"What the hell are you doing out here? Why are you following me?"

Her whisper cut the air, just as sharp as her mental voice, if quieter.

Despite my best efforts, a smile touched my face. I coughed to hide the smile before I answered her.

"You need my help. You're..."

Before I could tell her that she was going the wrong way, she flung her arms in the air again and put her finger in my face.

"I need *your* help? What am I, some helpless female in need of your strong, *manly* protection?"

The sarcasm and venom that dripped from her words actually stung a little bit.

"What I was trying to say was that you're going the wrong way. The nadrium is more to our north, and you're heading east!"

She laughed. Crossing her arms, she tilted her head just slightly to the left and smirked.

"This is why *you* need *me*, you lost little alien."

I'm not sure if it was the head tilt, the smirk, or the timber of her voice, but I couldn't help but enjoy the moment.

"Yes, the mineral you guys need is that way," she says, pointing to the north, "but the city it's in is heavily fortified and surrounded by a massive wall. We're not getting in there the normal way. I mean, look at you."

I looked at myself, then back at her. "What about me?"

"You're RED! You have scales! Humans don't generally trust their own kind, so the idea of just trusting a red, well-muscled, very good-looking..." she said those last three words in a sigh before clearing her throat. "...scaly alien is asinine. There's no way in any galaxy or universe they're just going to hand you the nadrium just because you ask for it."

"I'm not an idiot," I growled. "I have the holographic projector. As soon as we're near the city, I'll activate it."

"Great. So a total stranger comes to town, asking for

a valuable mineral for no reason he can explain. Are you going to try to buy it?" Her eyes narrowed. "What do you think they'll find of equal value? Who are you even going to ask?"

I pulled my hair in frustration. "This is why we need a plan, not to just go rushing in."

"I. Have. A. Plan."

Letting out a light sigh, I conceded that she might. Even if I didn't like it.

"If you do, mind telling me why we're headed in this direction instead?"

She shot me a look of disbelief. "We? So, you've just decided to come along with me?"

"I'm trying to keep you safe."

"Safe? I've been on this damn planet my entire life! I've been *alone* on this planet for years, and I *survived* without the help of your red lizard ass for that entire time. I think I can take care of myself."

"I'm not saying that you can't. But since you decided to bring up your *survival* tactics...Who in their right mind only uses a stun gun and a knife when fighting this planet? *You* did before we found you! *And*," I quickly said when she opened her mouth to respond, "do you really think one piddly little blaster is going to work against the Xathi?"

She clamped her mouth shut and glared at me. I could tell she was fuming, her mind-shield flicked in and out, giving me a rather broken and stuttered look into her thoughts.

"I could strangle you," she snarled.

I stepped closer to her, watched her eyes dilate, her breath catch. "I'd be willing to let you try," I murmured, "but I don't think it's going to end the way you're expecting." I glanced around. "Besides, it's muddy here. We'd get terribly dirty."

Jeneva spun, hands clutching at her short hair as if she'd pull it out, while I waited. She was strong. She was smart.

And if she thought I was letting her traipse through the jungle alone, she'd have to adjust.

"Fine," she grumbled. She didn't look happy, but she didn't have to be. She just had to be safe.

With smooth grace, she took the pack I offered her, strapped on the extra blasters and two of the knives I'd brought, and together we headed off to the east towards her mystery plan.

"I can feel other people," I said, scanning the forest.

I felt sadness, fear, and anger. Though some of that anger could have been from Vrehx. Actually, I was certain *all* that anger was coming from Vrehx.

"So what?" Vrehx huffed.

He was irritable, more so than usual. After what happened between us, I felt confused. But I think what happened between us was *exactly* what was making him angry.

Being with him made me feel good. I was able to forget about the Xathi invasion, my angry sister, and the pain of losing my parents. I thought Vrehx enjoyed it, too.

If he wanted to be upset about it, then that was his hang-up. Finding that mineral was the top priority, and at least one of us needed to be focused on that. I certainly wasn't in the mood to sit around on my ass until Vrehx and the others felt like doing something.

But I hadn't expected him to come after me.

"So, we should go see if they are okay," I replied.

"The *Vengeance* can't support any more refugees," Vrehx said sharply.

I spun around to face him.

"I'm not leaving people out here to die if I don't have to. I thought you felt the same way, but clearly I was mistaken," I snapped.

I turned on my heel and stormed into the forest. The people weren't far, but their makeshift camp was set up in a dangerous place. There was nothing to protect them if any of the native creatures, or the Xathi, attacked.

"Hello!" I called out, keeping my distance and letting myself stay camouflaged against the forest in case any of the survivors were on edge and trigger-happy.

"Show yourself!" a gruff-sounding man growled.

I stepped out of the undergrowth with my hands up.

"It's all right, I'm human," I said in a calm, even voice.

There were about fifteen of them in total. Between them, I counted around six weapons, though several of them had found thorny branches and heavy rocks to arm themselves.

"Are you from the city? Can we seek shelter inside?" a woman asked, her face streaked with dirt and blood.

Her eyes were large, as if she was still in shock from what she had seen. Duvest must really be tightening their security if they were turning away refugees.

"I'm not from Duvest," I said. "I'm trying to gain entry, as well."

"Then get out of here! You can't have any of our supplies. You can't have any of our food!" the first man bellowed.

"I'm not here for your supplies. I'm here to help."

From somewhere in the forest behind me, I sensed Vrehx. I was relieved he had the good sense not to reveal himself just yet.

"This place isn't safe enough for a permanent camp. You need to move to the cave systems to the west if you want to wait and see if the city will allow you to take refuge in its walls. Or...there's a ship a few miles south. There are other humans on board already with food and shelter. I can take you there."

"Those bug...things," the shaken women said, her voice trembling, "they rounded up people and took them to their ship. They sent you to trick us!"

As distrust and suspicion rippled through the small group, anyone who possessed a weapon raised it.

I kept my arms up, empty palms facing them.

"No, it isn't a Xathi ship. It's a ship belonging to

those who're *fighting* the Xathi, trying to save our world," I explained, but my words fell on deaf ears.

A cracking charge from a blaster whizzed past my ear and struck a nearby tree.

"Drive her out! We will not be slaves!" the man who shot at me screamed.

The small group dissolved into a frenzy of panic and aggression.

"Don't shoot, conserve your power!" the first man yelled, before lobbing a large rock at me.

"No, wait, you don't understand!" I pleaded, dodging a rock that would have otherwise hit my head.

"Restrain her!" another refugee demanded. "Take her weapons!"

Several of the bigger men from the group moved toward me, makeshift weapons at the ready. Another blaster fired, but this time it came from behind me. One of the refugees yelped and dropped his branch, which was now black and smoldering.

Vrehx appeared from the forest, weapon drawn. His sudden appearance set the frantic refugees off again. Another blaster strike hit the ground just in front of us.

"Get down," Vrehx instructed.

I ducked, making my body as small of a target as possible. I felt Vrehx's muscular arm wrap around my back as he guided me back into the relative safety of the forest. We moved quickly.

The refugees didn't pursue us, but I could still feel their pure panic.

"Well, that went well," Vrehx snarked as soon as he decided we were far enough away. He withdrew his arm. "Now you see why I didn't want to help them."

"You didn't want to help them out of spite, not because you knew they would attack," I replied, running one hand through my hair.

"It wasn't out of spite," he argued. "And what about you? Before, you couldn't stand to be around other humans. Now, you're obsessed with collecting more of them."

"You know why I avoided other people." I let loose an exasperated sigh. "And there's a big difference between wanting to avoid people and not wanting my race to die in an alien invasion. What is your problem?"

"I don't understand you," Vrehx said after a moment of consideration. "I am not accustomed to things I don't understand."

"Tell me what you want to know," I said with a shrug. "It's that simple. No need for all of this." I gestured at his aggressive stance.

He took a breath, relaxing some.

"All right," he agreed.

He turned to the forest, motioning for me to follow him. When I caught up to him, he was ready to talk.

"You're different from the other humans I've

encountered and not just because of your abilities. I don't understand what makes you different."

"The cave you found me in? Not that much different than my home. I've been living in the surrounding woods for over a decade now. I suppose I would be a little different after spending so long with minimal human contact," I answered honestly.

"Your sister is angry with your choice to live alone," Vrehx pressed.

I nodded.

"We grew up in Nyhiem, one of the largest cities on this world," I explained. "After our parents died, I made the choice to move to the smallest town I could find. She hated me for it. I told her it was because we needed a fresh start, but I lied. Being around so many people was getting harder and harder." I swallowed, throat tight, thinking about that time. "And everywhere I looked I was reminded of Mom and Dad."

"I'm sorry for your loss," Vrehx said. He sounded genuine.

"Thank you," I said. Unshed tears burned my eyes, but damned if I'd hide them. Mom and Dad deserved more. "It didn't matter in the end. I couldn't stay in the town, either. Amira felt completely abandoned, and I don't blame her. When we lost our parents, she needed me to step up and be her caretaker, and I failed her."

We didn't speak for several minutes. I wrapped

my arms around myself as I walked, eyes downcast. I had never told a living soul anything like that before.

I kept it all inside. I didn't know how to process the feeling, the relief, of being open with someone. It felt good, like a small weight had been lifted from me, but it was also scary.

"The weight of your guilt and your sorrow has made you different from the others," Vrehx said, breaking the silence first, and I was grateful for it. "I understand you better now."

"What about you?" I asked. With him knowing so many personal things about me, I felt naked and exposed. "It isn't fair that you have a better understanding of me than I have of you."

I laughed, but it felt forced.

"I, too, have suffered loss," he said.

I waited to see if he would say more, but he just kept trudging through the forest.

"Is that all I get?" I prodded.

He stopped short, nearly causing me to run into him. I was ready for him to tell me off for being nosy, but he just sighed.

"This isn't the first time I've encountered the Xathi," he said, his shoulders sagging. "They've been a concern in my galaxy for decades, but this is the first time they've ever been this aggressive."

"That's why you banded together with the Valorni and the K'ver?" I asked.

He nodded.

"The Xathi war started with small scattered attacks," he continued. "I still don't fully understand what they were doing. They didn't wipe out whole populations. My best guess is that those small attacks were some sort of twisted training method for new soldiers. They share a consciousness, but that level of coordination likely still requires some training. Or maybe they just did it for pleasure. I'll never know for certain."

"What happened?" I asked, gently placing my hand on his forearm.

His muscles twitched at my touch, but he didn't pull away.

"For whatever reason, they chose my home world," he said, his hands balling into fists. "It happened so quickly I hardly had time to do anything. It was chaos. Destruction for the sake of destruction. They didn't even collect slaves or resources like they normally would."

"That's horrible," I whispered.

His mental shields were lowering. I didn't know if he was doing it on purpose or not. I let my consciousness reach out to his, gently touching his mind.

The sorrow that filled me was almost unbearable.

He was in anguish.

"My family was caught in the slaughter," he said bitterly. "There wasn't even enough left of their bodies to bury them."

I squeezed his arm gently, at a loss for words.

"My mother, my father, and my little sister were taken from me, right in front of my eyes. From that point on, this war became extremely personal. I failed once. I will not fail again."

He stepped away from me. The air between us felt cold in comparison to his warmth.

He never mentioned a mate.

The knowledge brought on an unexpected swell of relief, instantly overtaken by guilt for even thinking about that in light of his confession.

"I'm sorry for all that you've lost," I said quietly. "Thank you for telling me."

His back was to me, shoulders rigid. I tried to reach out to his mind once more, but he'd shut me out completely.

"I won't allow myself to become distracted," he snapped, his voice cold.

I blinked, surprised by this sudden shift in mood. But before I could reach out to him, he stormed off into the forest.

"Wait, Vrehx!" I called after him. "Don't go that way! It isn't safe!"

VREHX

I heard Jeneva calling after me as I pressed deeper into the forest, undergrowth crackling under my boots. A small, persistent part of my mind knew that it wasn't appropriate behavior. We had a task to complete, after all.

But my thoughts swarmed with the past, with memories and pain better left forgotten.

I hadn't meant to let myself think so hard about my life before, or about my family, but something about Jeneva just seemed to bring it out of me: emotion, nostalgia.

The only way I was going to be able to clear my head was to get some distance between us, some quiet.

I needed to get myself under control—something I seemed to seriously lack in Jeneva's presence.

At some point, she had stopped calling. I noted the fact distractedly, assuming she had just given up. It didn't occur to me that there might have been good reason for her silence.

Of course it didn't. My thoughts were far away, back on Skota Capulus, back to another time. The ground seemed to shift below my feet, no longer feeling like the soft give of unfamiliar vines.

Instead, I felt the hard, packed earth of home. I could almost taste the inviting air.

I was so lost in the illusion, so completely enfolded in my own memories, I almost didn't see the first one move.

From the corner of my eye—there and gone so fast I almost could have imagined it—was the faintest flash of green. I slowed my movements, returning to the present with a jolt.

I was in a clearing, small and almost perfectly circular. Around me, the woods were completely quiet —unnaturally so. With slow, deliberate movements, I turned to take in my surroundings.

I was now sure that something had moved. Where it had gone, though, was another matter entirely.

Another flash of green had me turning the opposite way, my weapon instinctively appearing in my hand. I was no longer concerned with my own movement.

Clearly, whatever I had stumbled upon already knew I was there.

At that point, it was just toying with me.

The game didn't last long.

Clearly possessing no more patience than I, the creature showed itself in the next moment. Large green legs snaked from the cover of the trees, moving almost casually into the clearing. I looked in wonder upon my newest threat, feeling almost as fascinated as I was threatened.

Its claws sank into the soft ground beneath it, its fangs slowly dripping a liquid that one glance could tell you was toxic. It met my gaze levelly, apparently unperturbed by my intrusion here.

Frankly, I wasn't exactly unhappy to see it, either. Nothing brings your mind back to the here and now quite like the threat of death. In fact, a fight might have been exactly what I needed to clear my head.

"*Vrehx!*"

Her voice, half-whisper, half-yell, surprised me. I hadn't even noticed her approach.

I hesitated to turn, unwilling to give my opponent an opening.

"I'm fine, Jeneva."

I felt her appear at my side, her body practically humming with tension.

"We need to get out of here. Now."

I heard the panic creeping into her voice, the fear. It ate at me quickly. I hadn't meant to scare her or put her in danger—again.

"Go on, I'll be right behind you."

"Vrehx, you don't under—"

"I said I'm fine."

I redoubled my attention on the sickly green beast, feeling a smirk pull at my lips and welcoming it. With cold calculation, I continued to stare the monster down. Sure, the thing looked fearsome, but I've never been one to even think of backing down from a challenge.

That was, of course, until the rest arrived.

As if it was an organized attack, the plants around me began to shake, vines parting easily before the onslaught. At first there was one, then two, then three —each looking larger than the last. Faster than I could react, they crossed into the clearing, fangs dripping and claws digging impatiently at the soft earth.

It was only then that I realized the extent of my blunder. I had stumbled, loudly I might add, directly into some kind of breeding ground.

The menacing beasts examined us patiently, young and old, large and small—an entire family of monsters.

Jeneva's fingers flew to my arm, nails pressing roughly into my bicep.

"Vrehx…"

Without taking my eyes off the threat, I reached over to Jeneva, taking her wrist to pull her behind me. To my undying frustration, she resisted.

"What the hell?" she asked, her voice still a harsh whisper. "I don't need you to protect me, Vrehx!"

"Jeneva, just—"

"No way! You don't even know what they are. Maybe you should get behind *me*."

I shouldn't have glanced her way. I should have known better. It was just one more effect she had on me: She was hard not to look at.

I turned my head, offering her the barest moment of my reproachful expression.

It was a moment too long.

The second my eyes turned from the threat, they swarmed, countless barbed legs kicking up clouds of dirt as they ran toward us. There was no time to argue, not a second to reason. In the few moments until they were upon us, I grabbed Jeneva, yanking her roughly behind me.

Defiant to a fault, she still managed to thwart my plan, using the momentum to throw herself into a roll. She came up a few feet away, her blaster already pointed toward the nearest beasts.

"Avoid the—" she shouted, her words cut off by a teeth-rattling shriek.

I looked in wonder toward the swarming spiders,

watching as the bone-chilling call was picked up, echoed by each creature.

"The spit!" she finished, confirming my earlier theory.

Toxic, of course.

The creatures were mere feet away by this time. I positioned my feet, pointing my blaster at the nearest target.

It shrieked again, louder than the first—only this time, it wasn't just unpleasant noise.

A glob of venom flew from its horrific mouth, sailing quickly through the air between us. It landed with a plop onto my exposed bicep, quickly coating my scales.

I didn't notice the pain, not at first. The first thing I noticed was the smell, like charred meat. Then came the pain.

For all my training, I nearly dropped my own blaster. Heat, stronger than flame, began to course through my arm, searing ever deeper into my scales.

Acid. I should have known.

I gritted my teeth, tightening my hold on my blaster. I could deal with the damage later. First, I had to make sure we had a later.

Jeneva fired from her position, bright streaks lighting the clearing. I watched as the blaster hit the spider-things, watched as the deadly fire ran over them like water. They were immune to it, their exoskeletons taking the blasts with ease.

I reached down to my boot, grabbing for my knife, before the nearest beast could reach me.

It was close now, two feet at most, and looking hungry. If I missed, I'd be dinner for sure.

With a single calming breath, I drew my arm back, aiming my throw at a weak-looking spot near one of the monster's joints. I let it fly a second before it was on me.

The knife flew through the air in slow motion. My breath stilled in my chest. Then, finally, it hit home.

With a loud *thunk*, the knife pierced the creature, tearing through the meaty flesh.

It let out another shriek, the loudest yet, its leg rising from the ground in the fashion of all wounded animals. I re-aimed my blaster, sending a few shots into its hideous face for good measure, but the beast was already retreating, letting out the occasional shriek of pain as it went.

I heard a familiar *thunk* and turned toward Jeneva. Her hand hung empty in the air, a look of triumph on her face.

Following her line of sight, I noticed the handle of her own knife, now sticking out of another creature. Blood flowed easily from the wound, staining the ground a deep red.

I aimed my blaster at the newly injured spider and let loose a barrage of shots. As before, the creature shrieked its rage, turning quickly back to the safety of the forest.

The calls of the two injured spiders were heard even after they were no longer in sight. It seemed to have a strange effect on the remaining monsters. They stopped mid-stride, tilting their heads as if listening very closely.

Then, as sudden as they had appeared, they turned from us, following the cries of their injured peers.

After another minute of shrieking, silence finally descended around us, sounding almost eerie in the wake of such chaos. I turned to Jeneva, smiling broadly at her as she walked back toward me.

"What the hell were you thinking?" she scolded me as she neared.

"I—I wasn't. I'm sorry."

"You don't look very sorry."

With an effort, I forced the smile off my face. "I am."

She scoffed, her eyes rolling slightly before coming to rest on my arm.

"Oh, shit, Vrehx, did you get hit?"

I followed her gaze, "Well, I—"

"I told you to avoid the spit!"

"Well, you didn't say it was acid."

"Did I need to? 'Avoid the spit.' That was pretty clear."

"I just assumed it was poison."

She huffed in frustration. Her brow was furrowed, her lips downturned in a way that had my own eyes locked onto them.

Like I said, nothing to bring yourself back to the present like a brush with death. And presently, I was back to staring at a very attractive female.

"Come with me," she instructed, breaking my view of her mouth as she turned quickly toward the forest.

"Where are we going?"

She didn't answer, merely beckoned me on with an impatient flick of a wrist.

A few minutes later, we arrived at the opening of a cave, nearly hidden behind a curtain of thick vines.

"This way," she ordered, bending to fit into the entrance.

My blood pooled to my groin at the sight, and I followed quickly, not needing to be told twice.

The roof of the cave rose past the entrance, the thin corridor giving way to a circular chamber. It was cool inside, the space illuminated only by what light filtered in through the vines.

"Sit," she instructed, pointing to a seat-like outcropping.

"I'm fine, Jeneva."

She turned, her steely expression back in place.

I grumbled as I made my way to the stone seat, taking the time to shoot her an equally disapproving look before sitting.

She knelt before me, leaning in to inspect my injury.

"Why didn't the scales help?" she asked, not taking her eyes from my arm.

"Unfortunately, they only really help with sharp weapons and punctures, not chemicals or burns."

She nodded, running a single finger along the length of my bicep.

"Well, I'd say you got lucky. He must have been running low on acid. This will need to be bandaged, but it's nowhere near as bad as it could have been."

I felt her relief as she spoke, her mental blocks lowering in her worry. My already rushing blood turned hot, fire flowing through my veins.

The past was long gone. Jeneva was right here in front of me.

And this madness couldn't be denied.

Without thinking, I reached out to her, my fingers cupping the base of her skull as she looked up at me questioningly. Before she could ask, I pulled her to me, my lips crashing into hers, needing her taste more than any medicine.

She didn't hesitate, despite the anger I still felt

pouring off her. Her response was immediate. She kissed me hungrily, deeply, and I answered in kind.

Her legs came up to either side of me, straddling my lap as she lowered herself on me. I felt her desire and need as plainly as I knew she felt mine. My cock throbbed with it, the need to lose myself in her pleasure, her pleasure driving mine, spurring me on.

With gentle hands, she reached for my shirt, removing it slowly over my burnt arm. I winced as the fabric scraped along the injury. The expression mirrored in her face, our minds linked and tangled into one.

"Vrehx," she moaned, grinding herself against me as the fabric pooled on the floor. My hands dug into her hips, pulling her even closer, the press of her breasts into my chest sparking a desperate need to see more of her, touch more of her.

Her head fell back and I kissed down her throat, each tiny cry of pleasure sweetness to my soul.

"Please," she gasped, "I need, I want-"

More.

Hunger. Need.

Every molecule of my body demanded that I touch him, that he touch me.

He could have died. I'd never been so afraid when fighting the aramirions.

Never had so much to lose.

I nipped down his neck, fury and worry and heat mixed into a cocktail, a drug that kept me high, flying on his scent, his taste.

It occurred to me, as he nearly tore the shirt from my back, that we were defying some kind of natural order merely by being together.

The thought only served to fuel my desire.

I ground myself against him again, leaning in to take his mouth with my own. My barriers had fallen away completely, the focus required to keep them stable having been directed elsewhere. I felt his longing as if it were my own, felt the sharp sting as I took his bottom lip roughly between my teeth.

It should have been overwhelming—it nearly was. But just then, I discovered a whole new side to this "empathic" ability, one that didn't make me want to hide. One that brought me pleasure rather than pain.

Vrehx had done that for me. He had given me a hiding place, as well as a reason to come out of it. And fuck, was it ever a good reason.

He placed his hands on my pants, and I stood, pulling him up with me to better free ourselves of our constraints. In a flash, they were gone, added to the growing pile at our feet. He lifted me then, strong hands wrapping around my legs to pull me up and around him.

I gripped his arms hard, my nails digging into his scales as he walked slowly across the cave.

I could feel the pressure on his skin as if it were my own, my smooth flesh seeming to harden around me one moment, then softening again the next. I felt his cock throbbing against me.

I felt everything, and for the first time in my life, I didn't shy away from it.

I embraced it, letting the intensity of our touch wash over me in waves. We blurred in my mind until I could hardly tell one of us from the other. I didn't know if it was my back slamming against the cool stone of the cave wall, couldn't tell if it was my skin being kissed or his.

It quickly ceased to matter. Mine or his, our skin was on fire, smoldering under the intensity of our need.

His cock stood hard between us, the press of it against my core making me grind harder against him.

I glanced down, then blinked, the shock of it knocking me out of my fevered haze. Red. I'd expected that.

Wide and long. I'd felt that before, in his cabin.

Seeing the thick knobs ringing his cock, narrowing from base to tip was more than a surprise.

"How will this even work?" I whispered, then reached between us to glide my fingers down his length as it throbbed in sync with the rhythm of his heart.

The feedback from Vrehx's mind was immediate, overwhelming, pleasure an arrow aimed straight at my core.

He dipped his head, taking one of my hardened nipples between his lips.

I threw my head back, moaning in ecstasy as his tongue circled and pulled.

"Vrehx," I moaned, "now."

His hands tightened around my legs at my words, his head pulling up to look me in the eye. His gaze was pure passion and lust. His red eyes shone across me as if they were living flame.

No one had ever looked at me the way Vrehx did. No one had ever wanted me quite so badly.

"Jeneva," he returned, the word drawn out, sounding almost like a prayer. "I can deny you nothing."

And then he lifted me just enough that the tip of his cock pressed against my clit, slid between my lips. Inch after inch of his enormous cock filled me in slow motion, each knob crashing into my overstimulated bundle of nerves.

I threw my head back in amazement, nearly knocking myself out on the cave wall as I did.

I didn't care. I hardly even felt it.

How could I, after all, when I was already feeling so much? I could practically taste his pleasure as he thrust into my slick folds. I could feel his insatiable hunger for me.

His sensations mingled with my own, twisting and pooling within me until I felt I might explode from the sheer power of it all.

And still I wanted more, needed more. I wrapped my arms around his neck, hanging on for dear life as I thrust back against him. His cock slammed deeply into me, filling me in ways I had never thought possible.

My vision blurred, the world swaying around us. I didn't think it was possible for anyone to experience so much ecstasy, was sure I would explode any minute now from sheer delight.

And yet, I was also certain that that was a risk I was willing to take.

"Vrehx!" I cried, my fingers digging roughly into his shoulders.

My voice bounced off the walls around us, the sound amplified in the small space.

I could feel my orgasm building, heat spreading through me like wildfire. I moaned wildly into the darkness of the cave, feeling his own end drawing near.

"Srell, Jeneva," he groaned. "How do you do this to me?"

I didn't answer, couldn't answer. I only leaned forward, claiming his mouth with mine just as my orgasm began to rip through me.

We came together. A million sensations tore through my body and mind, pleasure too intense to ever name. My sight seemed to dim, and my hearing grew muffled.

All thoughts and all senses seemed to fade away—everything, that is, but the feeling of Vrehx, the sensation of what he was doing to me, and I to him.

I slumped against him as it passed, my body feeling completely devoid of energy. I wasn't alone. Vrehx actually seemed to sway on his feet before righting us.

"Srell," he repeated almost shakily.

I could barely nod. "Yep, you got that right."

He chuckled, his chest rumbling beneath me as he turned away from the wall and headed toward a flat space across the cave.

He carried me easily, his feet slapping against the ground as he went. I could hear the sharp echo of his movements, could feel his warm skin pressing against me, his arms cradling me.

I sighed into him, fully relaxing for the first time in as long as I could remember.

And then there was only darkness.

I woke to streams of light, errant rays pushing themselves through the thick cover of vines. I sat with a jolt, eyeing the cave in confusion. It wasn't until I caught sight of Vrehx that my memories began to sort themselves out.

He lay beside me, awake now, a questioning expression on his face.

"Are you alright?" he asked, sitting up slowly.

"Yeah, just forgot where I was."

My eyes traced his still naked body, the sun's weak rays playing beautifully along his scales. He looked like something holy in this light, like he glowed from within.

My core clenched at the sight, memories of last night flashing quickly through my mind.

I physically shook my head, trying to clear the rogue

thoughts. We were on a mission here: Get the mineral, save the world. There was no time for steamy cave sex.

"We should get going," I announced, standing and crossing over to my clothes.

I could sense his eyes on me as I walked, could feel his desire brush lazily across my mind. With a sigh, I put my barriers back into place, effectively blocking his wayward ideas.

"Come on, Vrehx."

He rose with a groan of defeat, following me over to our pile of discarded garments. We dressed in silence, trying our level best to keep our eyes off one another. It was a losing battle.

Somehow, though, we managed.

Several minutes later, we pressed our way back through the vines, stepping quickly back into the forest and the growing light of morning. I swept my eyes around slowly, checking for any signs of threat.

"Okay," I said, satisfied, "so we just need to—Vrehx, are you listening?"

He was looking away from me, his attention aimed at something overhead.

"What?" I turned, following his line of sight.

I didn't know how I had missed it.

Billowing above the trees, growing larger by the moment, was a dark cloud in the direction of the refugee camp that had driven us away.

"Smoke…"

I turned to Vrehx, finding his face in an expression I knew I wore myself.

The Xathi. Fuck.

We moved as one, both surging forward as if we had planned it, our feet propelling us through the trees. Somewhere, on some level I still didn't understand, I knew it was already too late.

But I pushed the thought away forcefully, clinging desperately to hope, any hope.

There was none to be found.

We skidded to a stop as we neared the settlement, our eyes raking over a now-familiar scene. It was as gruesome as before, as heart-wrenching. Bodies lay strewn along the ground, puddles of already congealing blood marking the path of destruction.

I walked slowly into the bloodbath, lowering my barriers as I went. There was nothing, no one.

No pain, no fear. Just the quiet misery of death, a tinge of fading desperation. We were too late, just as I had known we would be.

I swayed on my feet, and Vrehx was there, steadying me with one large hand.

"There's no one left," he said, his voice quiet.

I nodded, unable to bring myself to speak.

"Jeneva…"

I shook him off, stepping back from his infuriatingly calm demeanor.

"It—it's my fault," I choked out, shaking away the tears that stung my eyes.

"No," he said, his voice suddenly hard.

I ignored him completely. "I should have helped them. We should have been here!"

I was in a near-panic state, my hands trembling in anger and helplessness.

"No." He crossed to me, taking me briskly by the shoulders.

His eyes, still glowing in the pale light, seemed to bore into me. For a long time, he didn't move, didn't speak.

Then, "Don't you dare, Jeneva. It's not your fault. It could never be your fault. It's them, the Xathi. This is what they are. This is what they do. I refuse to let you blame yourself for them."

I shook my head, pulling back from his stare. Logically, I knew he was right, but my heart...

"We will stop them," he said, his voice heavy with promise. "Every last one of them. Somehow, we will make them pay for this."

Logic, emotion, reassurance... None of it had reached me. But at those words, I brought my burning gaze back to him.

Vengeance I could get behind—punishment for these atrocities, for the lives lost.

I nodded once, squaring my jaw in determination. He was right.

It was them. And we would make them pay.

Somehow.

"Good," he answered, releasing his hold on me. "Then, let's go."

VREHX

For a long time, I had blamed myself for the death of my family. I'd convinced myself that if I had done things differently during the Xathi attack, they would still be alive now. But the truth of the matter was they would have perished either way.

I just would have died with them.

For years, I wished that was what happened.

I've since realized that I can use my remaining years to avenge them, and perhaps even more importantly, ensure that what happened to my family will never happen to another.

It was *not* my fault my family was killed. It was the Xathi's fault.

It was *not* Jeneva's fault that the group of mad

humans perished. It was the Xathi's fault. It might take time for her to see it that way, though.

"Where exactly are you taking me?" I asked. She'd already told me once, but I needed to get her talking. Otherwise, she would get too wrapped up in her own head.

"I told you," she said, looking over her shoulder at me. "I might know someone who can help us. Maybe."

"Thank you for that incredibly vague answer," I quipped. "Are you purposefully trying to keep me in the dark?"

"I was going to earlier! But then I was a little bit distracted by the people trying to kill me with stones. Not to mention saving you from a nest of aramirions." I heard the smirk in her voice.

I was glad for it. I'd rather her tease me than be consumed by grief.

She looked over her shoulder at me again and smiled. I smiled back. I didn't even have to think about it. It was simply an automatic response to her.

She halted, letting me fall in by her side. She suddenly frowned and gave me a once over.

"What is it?" I asked.

"Now that I think about it," she said thoughtfully, "you should probably utilize your disguise. My friend, Renna, she's old and has seen a lot of shit—but I don't want to give her a heart attack by showing up with you in your true form."

"I feel as if I should take offense to that," I jested.

She rolled her eyes but still smiled. "You know I don't have a problem with this," she purred, tracing her fingers over the scale plating on my arm. An involuntary shudder ran up my spine.

"Keep that up, and we'll never make it to your friend," I said with a grin.

"So get on with it." She took a step back and I activated the holograph before gesturing broadly to my transformed body.

"Is this to your satisfaction?" I quipped.

She laughed. "You're still very handsome, if that's what you wanted to know," the lift of her lips taking any sting from her tone. "And you won't scare the life out of Renna, which is a big plus. Come on, we're nearly there."

We walked in companionable silence for approximately another half mile. The house was well camouflaged. I didn't see it until we were almost upon it.

Suspended roughly eight feet above the forest floor was a platform built between the trunks of four sturdy trees, which I assumed were not sentient in any sense of the word.

An old woman stood on the porch before a narrow

set of stairs that went down to the forest floor. Her ancient face was marred with worry. She wrung her papery hands.

I noted her appearance immediately. It was difficult to tell at first due to her advanced age, but she bore several of the same genetic markers as Jeneva. The shape of her cheekbones, the slope of her brow, and their noses—all were strikingly similar.

"Jeneva, is that you?" she called as we approached. She didn't wait for an answer. She hobbled down the stairs at a speed I wouldn't have thought possible, given her physical appearance.

She pulled Jeneva into a fierce hug despite the fact that Jeneva had several inches over her.

"Where have you been? I thought those…things got to you! Is your sister alive? Where is she? What's happening?"

Jeneva forced a laugh, her body stiff.

"I'm sorry I worried you, Renna," Jeneva said as she began to gradually relax. "Amira is alive. Though she's pretty pissed at me. But, then again, what else is new?"

"Who's this?" Renna asked, casting a suspicious look in my direction.

"This is Vrehx," Jeneva explained. "He's from a small settlement a few hours outside of Glymna. And he's a friend. He saved my life. And Amira's."

"That's a good recommendation," Renna said with a

kind smile. "Come in and sit. You both must be exhausted. Jeneva, why don't you eat more? I could snap your bones if I tried."

Jeneva simply laughed and followed the old woman into the cottage.

The cottage was small, clearly designed for a solitary life. Everything inside had been made from something in the forest. Renna offered both myself and Jeneva the only chair in the small front room.

After we both refused it several times, Renna sunk her body into the chair. Her bones creaked as her weight shifted.

"Renna, have you been taking your tonic?" Jeneva asked, giving the old woman a reproachful look. Renna's face was full of mischief. "That's it! I'm making you some right now." Jeneva stood up and strode to the far side of the room that served as the kitchen.

"Don't bother. I'm all out of verdane extract," Renna called out.

Jeneva gave the woman an exasperated look. "There's a grove nearby. I'm going to get some for you," Jeneva said, her jaw set in determination. "How do you expect to live forever if you don't take care of yourself?" she admonished.

She then turned to me. "I know some grows very close to here. Less than 10 minutes fast walking. If I'm not back in twenty minutes, come look for me."

I moved to join her. I didn't like the idea of her out in this forest alone, no matter how skilled she was at surviving in it.

Renna put a hand on my arm, stopping me. "Do keep me company while she's gone," Renna said. "I rarely get visitors out here. I never get to meet new people."

Jeneva gave me a smirk before dipping outside.

"Not much of a talker, are you?" Renna teased after we spent several minutes sitting in silence.

Srell.

If I spoke in my native tongue, my disguise would be futile. My only option was to test out my grasp on the human language. Luckily, my prolonged time with Jeneva had made the neurotransmitter's job much easier.

"You are a relative of Jeneva?" If I spoke in simple sentences, I should be able to avoid raising suspicion.

Maybe.

"I've always suspected as much," Renna said with a shrug.

"You mean you don't know for certain?" Humans and their social bonds were perplexing, to say the least.

"I left my family behind long ago," Renna explained. "We lived in a large city. My husband, myself, three daughters, and two sons." I did not know if that was considered a large family or not, so I just nodded.

"The city affected me strangely," Renna continued. "I would get headaches, but very unusual ones. I wanted to leave the city, to move someplace quieter.

"My husband refused. I stayed as long as I could stand it, for my children. But in the end, I had to do what was best for me. I came out here. And I've been happy. But I never stopped missing my children."

"Where does Jeneva fit into that?" I asked.

"I make a living as a liaison between poison harvesters and buyers in town. Jeneva is one of the best gatherers I've ever come across. And, the first time I met her I felt something. She felt just like one of my daughters had," Renna sighed, a sadness seeping into her eyes. "I don't know, I can't know. But I'm still sure of it."

"You can feel the emotions of others? You're an empath?" I asked.

"I didn't know there was a fancy name for it. What I can do isn't anything fancy," Renna laughed. "Sometimes I can sense feelings in others. Sometimes I can't. It isn't anything more complicated than that."

"Does Jeneva know anything?" I asked. With the strain between her and her sister, it might do Jeneva good to know she has another family member—or even someone who shares her abilities.

"She doesn't know I'm her grandmother, and she doesn't know about my abilities," Renna shook her head. "I think the best thing I can do for her is to be exactly what I am."

I nodded, not fully understanding—but it wasn't my place to interfere.

"What are we talking about?" Jeneva said as she pushed open the door with her hip.

She was carrying an armful of the most brilliantly green plant I had ever seen. And that was really saying something, considering we were in the middle of a forest.

"I was just about to tell your friend here about being one of the first people ever born on this world," Renna said smoothly.

"You were?" I asked, playing along.

"Indeed I was. You should have seen this place back then," Renna sighed dreamily. "It was a paradise. The original settlers brought over so many pictures of the old Earth, but anyone would have sworn those pictures were taken here."

"So much water, so much greenery, gorgeous mountains," Renna mused. "Even the planet's rotation was almost identical to the old Earth's. Of course, it would have been better if their original surveys had recognized how alive the forest really was." Her mouth twisted in a wry smile. "Not exactly the Eden they had hoped for. But we found ways to survive and eventually thrive."

Pride shone on Renna's face for a moment—before it darkened. "But with those horrible creatures falling from the sky, I don't know what's going to happen."

"That's actually why we are here, Renna," Jeneva said, walking over to stand near the old woman. "We've come to ask for your help."

JENEVA

I could not have survived in the wilds without Renna - in more ways than one.

While I lived in complete solitude, I had to earn some sort of living. Sure, my home was made from materials I foraged. And I ate what I could find in the forest as I was too far away from any town to regularly stock up on food.

But my gear, my med supplies, and, eventually, my harvesting equipment—they all had to come from town. Which meant I needed income.

It was Renna who first taught me how to harvest poisons. She found me in the forest years ago after I'd collapsed from being exposed to sorvuc toxins.

It was sheer luck. She helped me recover, taught me about each plant and creature of the vast forest, and showed me how to extract valuable poisons and venoms. She saved my life, and gave me a career of sorts.

All I had to do was bring what I gathered to her, and she would handle the rest.

I didn't know a lot about her end of the business, but I knew she had contacts in every city.

"Can you get us into Duvest?" I asked.

Renna blinked in surprise.

"This is the first time you've ever wanted to go to a city," she said, eyebrows raised.

"It's important." I bit my lip, wondering how much I could say. The more I told Renna, the more likely it was that she would discover Vrehx was actually from the other side of the rift.

"I have a relative in Duvest," Vrehx said quickly.

I tried not to let the shock register on my face. His language skills weren't perfect, but certainly improving faster than I had realized.

"I am anxious to see if they are all right, but it has been so long since I've visited, I'll be a stranger to the guards."

"That's right," I added, a small tightness in my throat. Lying was never my forte. I didn't spend enough time around people to learn how to be a good liar. And even if I *had* been a good liar, Renna wasn't someone I wanted to lie to.

"Hmmm...Many of the guards dabble in the poison harvesting business to make a little extra on the side," Renna said.

I don't know if she bought our lie or simply elected not to press further. Either way, I was grateful.

"When you approach the entrance to the city, tell the guard 'Lymirai.'"

"The death flower?" I asked, perplexed.

"It's my favorite," Renna shrugged. "If the guard has done business with me, they'll recognize the term. Once you're inside, look for my buyers. You've met them before."

"Where?" I asked, puzzled. Meeting people was never on my list of things to do. Surely I'd remember strangers.

"They've been here at the cottage several times while you've dropped things off for me," Renna explained.

"Those were your *buyers*? I always thought they were just couriers or something.," I said.

If I concentrated, I could remember their faces. I would probably recognize them if I saw them again.

"Well, that's what assuming will get you," Renna tutted. "My oldest buyers come to visit from time to time. Work with someone long enough, and you get to be friends. If you tell them I sent you, they will help you."

I nodded, waiting for more.

"Tobias and Shad know everything and everyone in Duvest. A pair of bright boys, tinkering with all sorts of things now. I'm sure finding your relative will be no problem for them."

"Thank you," I said. "I hate to leave so soon, but we don't have much time to spare."

"Of course, dear," Renna said with a sweet smile. She rose to her feet on slightly unsteady legs. I hurried to her side to help her up.

"If I..." I trailed off. I didn't know how to say it. My eyes stung from unexpected tears. "If I don't see you again..."

I couldn't. I couldn't make myself say it. Renna reached up and patted my cheek with her wrinkled hand.

"You're a good girl, Jeneva," she murmured. I put my hand over hers and stood for a moment.

"Goodbye, Renna," I said before hurrying out of the cottage. Renna always understood.

"ARE YOU ALL RIGHT?" Vrehx asked when he caught up to me.

"Yes," I lied. I couldn't let my emotions get the better of me now. We had to get to Duvest.

Vrehx might never move like he was born here, but he was improving, and we made good time getting through the forest. It had been years since I laid eyes on the city, but it looked nothing like I remembered.

A thirty-foot-high electric force field encircled the city. All entrances had been shut down except for one— and it looked anything but welcoming.

Armed guards were everywhere, barricades constructed from sheet metal, shipping crates— basically anything they had on hand, from the looks of it.

We approached a guard's station set up near the city's remaining entrance and I tested my mental blocks. If we were going to pull this off, letting the fears and panic of a city's worth of minds into my head wasn't going to help.

"The city is closed," he said before I had a chance to speak. "We have nothing to give you. You'd best move along."

"We aren't refugees," I said, gritting my teeth. "And every person you turn away is a person you're sending to their death." My voice rose in pitch as the images from the burned-out camp covered my vision.

Vrehx touched my arm. "Jeneva," he said gently, bringing me back to the here and now.

I took a deep breath, forcing my anger to cool. I

couldn't make a scene. We had to get in and out as soon as possible.

"Lymirai," I said to the guard. He blinked once.

"Pardon?"

"Lymirai," I repeated, slower this time. Something hard came into the guard's eyes. His upper lip twitched.

"I don't know what that means," he said stiffly. He casually rested his hand on his gun.

Liar, I thought. But I didn't say anything. Maybe the guards that ran their own sidelines had been found out, purged. Maybe this one really didn't know what I was talking about, and was just suspicious of everyone.

"All right," Vrehx said, taking a step back. He was not retreating, simply showing the guard we were not a threat. "You don't know what that means. But perhaps you can still help us. We're looking for two men."

"Their names are Tobias and Shad, do you know of them?" I added.

The guard's expression changed suddenly. "You're a friend of Tobias and Shad?" he asked. I swore I could see fear in his eyes.

"Renna sent us with a message for them," I said. "If you won't let us in, I need you to bring them out."

"I'll send someone for them," the guard said, walking away with renewed vigor.

"What was that about?" Vrehx asked.

I shook my head, at a loss. I wasn't going to question

the guard's change of heart. Something in his eyes told me I didn't want to know. Surely Renna's friends weren't that scary, right?

Fifteen minutes later, two men approached the guard station.

One was tall, dressed completely in white, with sunbaked skin and black hair shot through with silvery white. The other, not as tall but twice as muscular, had a mean look on his ruddy face and wore an unfamiliar military uniform. It didn't match anything the guards wore.

"I remember you," the taller one said in a clipped voice.

"Jeneva," I supplied awkwardly.

"Shad," he extended a tan, long-fingered hand. I shook it gingerly, careful that my mental door stayed closed before I touched him.

"Renna send you?" The other one, Tobias, grumbled.

"Yes," I confirmed. "She said you might be able to help us."

"Come inside, and we'll talk," Shad said, cordially offering me his arm.

"Your friend will have to stay outside," Tobias said, folding his thick arms over his chest.

"No." I recoiled from Shad and stepped back towards Vrehx.

"Look, little girl," Shad said with an ice in his voice

that was twenty times more intimidating than Tobias's glare. "We don't take kindly to strangers right now. We've got the safety of the city to think about."

Crap. They really were that scary. They might have started doing business with Reena when they were just herbalists and tinkers, but from the looks the guards shot us, these two wielded serious power in the city.

I lifted my chin and looked Shad in the eye. "Renna sent both of us," I said pointedly. "We're a package deal. If you aren't okay with that, then I'll just have to go back to Renna's cottage and tell her—"

"Fine." Shad held up a hand quickly. "If Renna trusts him, then I do, as well." He turned to Vrehx with open arms. "Welcome, *friend*."

Vrehx looked like he wanted to shoot Shad between the eyes. Thankfully, he kept his temper in check as we were led through the entrance into Duvest.

The city was in a state of high alert. Guards were patrolling every street. Posted signs asked for volunteers and donations and gave warnings about conserving food and water.

Tobias and Shad led us into a derelict building. I balked at the entrance, but Tobias nudged me forward, down a short, utilitarian hallway, and then another door.

The inside of the building was the complete

opposite of the outside: gleaming wooden floors, plush furniture, and beautiful pieces of art.

"Wow," I breathed.

"Impressive, isn't it?" Tobias grinned.

"It's quite the collection," I agreed. If I ever moved back to a proper city, perhaps I would join the manufacturing business. I had no idea it could be so lucrative.

"Now," Shad said, sinking into a red velvet chair. Next to it on the side table was a holographic death flower bloom. I chuckled dryly at the sight of it. "What is it you needed?"

I should have thought this through better. Between seeing Reena, my exhaustion with Amira and the distraction of Vrehx, I'd just hoped for the best.

That had never really worked out.

"I need an item. A hard to get item. Renna thought you could help."

"You might have noticed we're in a bit of a lock down," Shad shrugged. "Aliens, invasion, all that." He leaned back into his chair. "Normal business is suspended for the duration."

"This might help get you back to normal business sooner." Maybe. I hoped. I looked around at the room, the luxury contained within. "I'd imagine the current state of affairs can't be profitable."

"You'd be surprised what we can make a profit out

of," Tobias laughed. "But now I'm curious. What exactly do you need?"

I took a deep breath. "Nadrium. About five pounds of refined nadrium."

They shot each other a look, leaned forward in their chairs.

"That's a very expensive favor, even for a friend of Renna's," Tobias finally said.

"And a potentially dangerous one," Shad added, rubbing his chin. "Why do you need it?"

"There's a good chance it will help against the invading creatures," I answered, minding my words. The less detail, the better, right?

"A good chance, you say?" Tobias joined in. "What makes you say that?"

"I have it on good authority from experts, who are friends of mine," I said. Though I kept my expression even, I cursed myself for how clumsy I sounded.

"Is *he* one of your experts?" Tobias jerked a thumb in Vrehx's direction.

"He is an associate, yes," I said. Panic rose in my throat. I couldn't keep this up much longer.

"Renna is a dear friend," Shad said, lacing his fingers together. "However, we do not know you. And you don't seem to be particularly forthcoming with information."

"Well, I don't know you, either. And I will not give out highly sensitive information so easily," I snapped.

Tobias stood, face reddening. "You come in here, waving Renna's name about. We've seen you, but never this guy. You want an expensive, explosive element, but won't give any information." He lunged forward, his meaty hand gripping my arm. "You sound like a spy to me. How do we know you're not a collaborator with the damn enemy?

Tobias shook me once, hard. "Start talking, or we'll splatter your brains on the wall," he growled.

Vrehx was on his feet in an instant, his hand clamping down on Tobias's shoulder, ripping him away from me.

"Don't touch her. Or else we will see what *I* can do to *your* brains," Vrehx growled.

Tobias jabbed his elbow back, his blow landing hard on Vrehx's hip.

There was a crunch, followed by an electric hiss. I watched, mouth open in horror, as Vrehx's holographic disguised flickered and failed completely.

Well...shit.

VREHX

Well, srell.

Jeneva's look of shock and the wide-eyed wonder on Tobias' and Shad's faces confirmed what I feared: the holographic disguise unit had failed.

"What in the hell?" Shad asked as he stumbled half a step backwards.

I let go of Tobias as he released of Jeneva and put my hands up in an attempt to calm the situation. "Okay. Let's take it easy," I said, trying to keep my voice as calm and sincere as possible.

Tobias looked between Jeneva and me. It was easy to see him trying to put things together.

"What in the holy hell is that?" he asked Jeneva as he pointed at me.

"Well, he's..." She was stumbling over her words,

trying to explain who—and what—I was. I decided to explain myself instead.

"My name is Vrehx. I am known as a Skotan, and I am part of a fighting force trying to defeat the Xathi."

"Xathi?" Shad asked.

As I opened my mouth to answer, Jeneva spoke up. "The crystal bugs that are attacking the cities. Vrehx and his people followed them here to try and stop them. They're how I know about the nadrium."

Shad took a seat while Tobias headed over to the far side of the room and poured himself a drink from a crystal carafe. Drinking the entire glass in one shot, he looked at me.

"You're fighting those things?"

I nodded.

"Why?"

I took a deep breath, wondering exactly how much I should tell them. It wasn't much of a decision.

"They destroyed my home world, killing my family in front of my eyes. My shipmates have all suffered similarly."

"And the nadrium is going to help you get rid of them?" he asked, eyes narrowed. "How?"

"Our ship was damaged when we came through the rift." I weighed my words. "The nadrium will restore power to damaged sections, as well as provide shelter to the human refugees we have already taken on board." I hoped that the mention of the survivors on the *Vengeance*, ones that Duvest would have turned away, would knock my inquisitors off-balance. No such luck.

Shad suddenly glared at me and sat forward on the couch. "What are you not telling us?"

"Nothing."

"Don't try to bullshit me, red. I'm a professional liar. You're hiding something. If you want our help getting the nadrium instead of calling the guards, you're going to tell us everything you know about those damn bugs. Why are they here? Hell, why are you here?"

"If I tell you the truth, you will get us the nadrium." I made it a statement instead of a question. I needed to ensure the retrieval of the mineral, no matter what.

"Deal," Tobais snapped. Shad shot him a look, but nodded in agreement.

"Very well. The Xathi are a hive-mind race. They invade worlds looking for food, fuel, and racial purity."

"Racial purity?"

"They wipe out anything that does not meet their standards. They've destroyed entire races, entire species. The only way to stop them is to eliminate the queens and sub-queens, but they are protected and rarely ever vulnerable enough to kill. They attack ruthlessly and without mercy."

Memories of their attack on my home flooded my

mind. Jeneva's hand in mine let me know my distress must have leaked out, brushing her mind.

"When they invaded my home, there was little that we could do. The Xathi soldiers swarmed over us. I fought them, trying to protect my siblings and parents, yelling at them to get into hiding."

My heart raced, still hearing the screams of my family.

"They died anyway. Planet after planet in our sector fell. The survivors formed an alliance. We've fought them to a stand-still, but never pushed them off a world they'd taken."

Something like sympathy flickered across Shad's face. His partner remained unconvinced. Fine. I'd lived through it once. Telling the story couldn't hurt me now.

"I ended up on board a ship called the *Vengeance*. Every member of the crew has lost their families, lost everything to the Xathi. Every one of us wants them permanently eliminated from the universe."

Tobias' eyebrows rose. "Sounds like genocide to me. Isn't that what they've done to your homeworlds?"

My lips twisted. "Tell me you don't want revenge for what they've done here." I waved my hand towards the city outside this glittering nest the two men had made. "Trust me. They haven't even gotten started."

He leaned back, considering, so I continued.

"We had a weapon aboard the *Vengeance*, a

prototype. Nothing had been able to penetrate a Xathi hull before. The queens and subqueens remained secure. Unstoppable. We had to reach them, whatever the cost."

Jeneva pulled her hand away from me. I could see it on her face—she was putting things together. She was starting to guess why the Xathi were here.

Shad and Tobias ceased to exist for me. I focused only on this woman who had somehow captured me deep within. I took a step towards her, reached out to her, but she pulled away.

"You brought them here." Her whispered voice shook. "All of this, it's because of you."

"We didn't know what the weapon would do! We were nowhere near this planet. We don't even know where in the cosmos we are!"

"Wait, wait-wait-wait-wait-wait-wait. Wait!" I ignored Shad, searched for a flicker of understanding on Jeneva's face.

Nothing. She had closed herself off to me. Had learned her lessons too well.

Shad pushed towards us. "What are you trying to say?"

"When we fired the weapon, it…" I try to control my breathing, but this time my discipline failed. "It tore a hole in space, bringing us and the Xathi ship through. It destroyed half of their ship, but the other half fell through the hole, got caught up in your planet's gravitational pull, and crashed to the ground.

"We fell with it. The trip through the hole damaged our engines. That's why we need the nadrium. If we can get the *Vengeance* back into space even if we can recharge our weapons, we can eliminate their threat to your planet."

Tears formed in Jeneva's eyes. I took a step towards her, but she threw her hands up to stop me. She backed away from me, shaking her head in denial.

I fought past the tightness in my throat, talking to the men but never taking my eyes off her.

"We need the mineral before they destroy your planet. With the *Vengeance* operational, we can actually keep things running. That means we can keep fighting and taking in more survivors. Which means not sitting here, waiting to be slaughtered."

"How do you know?" Tobias asked.

"Their subqueen is aboard that ship. With her dead, all of the Xathi on the planet will become inert. Based on how far our engineer thinks we are from the nearest queen, these Xathi will be unable to establish a connection with her and will simply stop moving. We can destroy them easily then."

I took another step towards Jeneva. "I'm sorry. We didn't know what would happen."

Her head snapped up, her eyes glaring at me.

Before she could speak, explosions rocked us all to our knees.

I rushed outside, grabbing my pack from next to the door. The whine of Xathi sleds shrilled amidst explosions, shouts, and screams.

Tobias and Shad were in the hallway behind me. "Get back inside! Get any weapon you have and get—"

An explosion nearby interrupted me. I looked to my left, and my heart froze for a very long second.

Four Xathi soldiers marched down the street, the click-clack of their claws on the pavement echoing louder than the background sounds of battle and death. A quick look back showed an empty doorway.

Good. The two men had taken Jeneva to safety. I was sure those two had more than one way out of their nest.

I pulled out my blasters, grim determination in my mind.

She may never forgive me, but I'd take out as many as I could. As many as I needed to ensure they never threatened her again.

"Vrehx!" I screamed.

I hated that my knee-jerk reaction was to call for him. I hated him.

Didn't I?

The explosions, the death, the Xathi—*he* did this. He brought war to my home world.

I was such an idiot. I can't believe I trusted him. I can't believe I trusted *any* of them.

But it was an accident, a small voice in the back of my mind whispered. He was fighting now to protect us. To protect me.

With a sob I clawed at my ear. Their damn device was still lodged in my ear. Despite every other horrible thing happening in that moment, all I could think about was getting that ear *thing* out of my body. I thrashed desperately, but a wall of pain slapped me back to stillness.

Right. A building just fell on me.

The entire gilded interior room had collapsed on us.

I listened for sounds of the others, but all I could hear was an endless hollow ringing. I was seeing double. I closed my eyes for a moment, willing the world to stop spinning.

Then it hit me.

The terror, the pain, and the confusion of every citizen in the city—slamming into my consciousness at the same time.

A low moan of agony escaped my lips.

"Close the door, close the door, close the door," I muttered to myself. To anyone listening to me—if anyone in this building was even alive anymore—I likely sounded insane. Perhaps I *had* gone insane.

I don't think anyone would blame me if I did. I took slow, shuddering breaths in an effort to calm my frantic mind, then slowly, carefully, opening it just a crack.

There they were. Tobias and Shad were still alive. The energy pulsing from their minds felt exactly like them, oily and shady.

"Hello?" I called out, my voice raw. "Tobias? Shad? Can you hear me?"

"I hear you," Tobias's gruff voice came from

somewhere to my right. The rubble shifted. His thick arm, bruised and bleeding, came into view.

"Where's Shad?" I asked.

"He's over here, too," Tobias said with a note of sadness in his voice.

"He's only unconscious," I said.

"How do you—"

"I feel his mind. It's a thing I do. Help me up." I lifted an arm for Tobias to grab, too tired to explain further.

"Did you just say you could *feel* his mind? That's impossible," Tobias grumbled as he hauled me to my feet.

"Right now, aliens are attacking your city. Care to define impossible a little more carefully?" I snapped.

The world spun on its axis, but eventually the walls all ended up in the right place. Well, except for the fallen parts. Those stayed firmly collapsed.

A groan came from the rubble where I 'felt' Shad.

"You should probably go help him," I said with a tight smile. Tobias hurried to the rubble pile to free his partner.

"Where's your alien friend?" Tobias spat as he hauled a sputtering Shad upright.

"For the record," I gestured wildly at the wreckage, "*this* is why I needed that damn nadrium. But *you* assholes had to be stingy about it!"

"And we were right in doing so!" Tobias argued.

"You heard that alien! He fired the weapon that brought those other aliens here. For all we know, it was all planned, and they're working together!"

I slumped against the rubble, blinking. Vrehx hid so much from me that, for all *I* know, he *was* working with the Xathi. Maybe everyone on the *Vengeance* was.

Maybe... I'd led my sister to a trap.

But I'd felt him, felt his mind in mine. Surely that had to count for something?

Another shuddering boom echoed through the city, interrupting my spiraling thoughts.

"Shit!" came a strange voice.

Tobias and I looked at one another, then to where the noise had come from. A man stumbled forward, catching himself on a jagged piece of concrete.

"You okay, Mac?" Tobias called.

"Just peachy, T," Mac replied, spitting blood. "A few others survived the collapse, too, in case you cared."

"Good to hear," Tobias said, either not registering, or ignoring, Mac's sarcastic tone. I assumed Mac and the small handful of survivors were other associates of Tobias and Shad's. Just as friendly and nice.

"Can we get a hand here, T?" Mac asked, looking over his shoulder at something I couldn't see.

"Mine are full at the moment," Tobias looked at Shad, who was leaning on Tobias for support.

Mac disappeared. There was a good deal of shuffling and groaning. I heard at least two other male voices in addition to Mac's.

From outside, I could hear the hum of the Xathi sleds and the crackle of their charged whips mixing with the panicked cries of the people. Before I could warn anyone, another thunderous boom echoed through Duvest. The rubble shifted, and more pieces of ceiling came crashing down.

"We've got to move before what's left of this building comes down on us," I said in a rush. "I don't think we'd survive it twice."

Tobias and I helped Shad, who was still disoriented, towards a gap of natural light.

"Whatever you do," I whispered as we neared the street, "don't let any of the Xathi see you. If one sees you, they all see you—and you won't escape. When Vrehx said they were hive-minded, that's what he meant." If I could trust what he'd told me...

I signaled for Tobias to wait out of sight behind the remaining half of a wall. He passed it on to Mac and the others. I wasn't particularly keen on them joining us, but I wasn't about to leave them behind, either.

Slowly and silently, I peeked out into the street. The Xathi were corralling civilians, using electrified whips to keep them from escaping. Nausea churned in my stomach as I thought of the fate of those poor people. With tears in my eyes, I turned back to Tobias and Shad, who seemed a little more alert now.

"We can't go that way. Xathi are collecting people to take as slaves. Or food," I muttered. Tobias looked pale. I couldn't tell if Shad understood any of what was going on. "You know the city inside and out. We need a place to hunker down and hide until I think of a plan."

"Why are *you* coming up with a plan?" Tobias sneered.

"Why? Are *you* going to do something about this?" I said, jerking my head in the direction of the Xathi.

"Fuck no, I'm not," Tobias exclaimed. "I'm going to survive. And if you want to try to fight those creepy sons of bitches, you can count me out." Shad groaned in agreement. "Count *us* out," Tobias corrected.

"Us, as well," Mac said, gesturing to the surly men that were following him.

"You're all useless," I muttered. "Just take us somewhere safe." And I'd decide on a plan when I was there, even without these cowards.

Tobias supported Shad, while Mac and his men followed. I brought up the rear. I looked over my shoulder every other second, looking for Xathi.

And maybe, just a bit, for Vrehx.

I shouldn't care if he was dead or alive, but I did. I

couldn't help it. I reached out with my mind, but I couldn't feel him. The overwhelming panic in the city was just one big tangled mess in my mind.

Why should I care about Vrehx?

But even as my mind formed the thought, I knew I didn't mean it. His betrayal was a fresh wound, and it ached. I hoped he was alive, but that didn't mean I forgave him.

Something on the ground caught my eye. A glint of blue. I stepped closer, hoping it was what I thought it was. I kicked some debris aside and smiled. It was part of a Xathi leg, blown off at the joint by its own bomb.

"Serves you right," I mumbled to the leg as I scooped it up. The fragment was about the size of my arm. If I recalled correctly, Vrehx said the Xathi hunters were blue.

I kept it. Vrehx had used a limb as a club before.

To protect me.

I couldn't turn down any weapons, no matter how grisly.

Even now, my mind still circled to him. I reached out for him again, but nothing. Fingers of ice gripped my chest.

Eventually Tobias brought us to a building that looked just as dilapidated as the one we came from. Further away from the city center, the attack had done some damage, but there were no signs of life anywhere, human or Xathi.

"What is this place?" I asked, stepping through a doorway that was missing its door. Mac and his men made themselves at home, picking through the rubble and examining anything they thought had value.

"Old manufacturing plant," Tobias replied, propping Shad against a wall. "Cheap to run."

"Is he okay?" I asked. Shad's eyes roamed the room, not focusing on anything.

"I think he's in shock. He did almost die an hour ago," Tobias shrugged. "I've done lots of things, but never was a medic."

I looked around, mind reaching for any start of a plan, anyway we could strike back. "What sort of plant was this?" I asked.

"Oh, all sorts of stuff," Tobias said, seemingly grateful for something resembling a normal conversation. "Last time it was up and running, it specialized in sonic tech. Shad owns this one. Real fascinated with sonic stuff, he is," Tobias nudged Shad, who gave a nod of agreement. When this was all over, he really needed to see a doctor.

If it was over.

If we could find one.

"Not just sonic," Shad murmured. His words were a bit slurred, but coherent. "The manufacturing end kept this place in profit. But the real magic happened in the labs."

"Is that right?" I asked. I wanted to keep him talking. If he was talking, he wasn't dying, right?

"Imagine a howler that didn't just use sound to drive a creature away but actually disrupted their brain activity."

I grabbed his hand, forced his attention back to me. "What did you just say?"

"Using sonic frequencies to disrupt the brain activity of hostile wildlife?" Shad repeated.

"Yes! Did it work?" I demanded. My mind was whirling. Thoughts chased after each other at a mile a minute.

"Did what work?" Shad asked with a dazed smile.

My face fell. For a moment there, I thought we might actually have a bit of luck. But if Shad was too confused to focus, we'd never get anywhere.

"He was obsessed with those things for months," Tobias sighed. "There's probably a whole bunch of them in here still."

I sat up immediately.

"Where?" I asked.

"Well, the lab would have been back through that way," Tobias said, pointing at a corridor that didn't look entirely safe but was still passable. "Why? The regular howlers barely work; I doubt those things would do anything."

"If I found some, would Shad know how to adjust the frequency?" I continued.

"He sure would," Tobias said, his confusion only deepening. "But in the state he's in now, I don't know if he *cou*—"

I was off and running before he could fully finish his sentence, returning several minutes later with an armful of howler prototypes.

I knelt in front of Shad and held one up to his face.

"Oh!" he said, his eyes brightening. "You've found one of my projects! This is going to change everything, you know?"

"Yes, I do," I said intently. "If you can help me with this, your invention will change the world and save a lot of lives."

"Hello," he blinked. "Have we met?"

I rolled my eyes. "Take this," I said, pressing a prototype into his hand. "Mess with the sonic frequencies until it does something to this." I held up the blue crystalline leg.

Shad went to work right away. Apparently, howlers were relatively simply devices. He adjusted the frequencies. Many so quiet, my ears couldn't detect them. Some so low I felt them vibrating through my chest. A few made my ears feel like bleeding.

I was beginning to lose hope when I felt the leg start to tremble in my hand.

"It's working!" I exclaimed. Shad's focus was clear as he slowly adjusted the sonic frequency.

The leg hummed so violently, I had to set it down.

Then it cracked.

VREHX

I ducked behind some rubble, grunting in pain as my knee almost buckled again.

I cursed my own stupidity, thinking I could hurdle straight over one of the Xathi. It'd almost worked. That one and its squad were dead, but I couldn't afford any more stupid mistakes.

I rubbed my left knee and instantly regretted it—the pain was intense. I pushed the pain aside and peered around the rubble.

A dozen Xathi were rounding up citizens, and there wasn't a damn thing I could do about it.

It had been maybe ten or fifteen minutes since the explosions had first started. The Xathi that I had first attacked were all lying in pieces a few blocks away, one of my blasters in fragments, lying in a puddle of blood next to them.

I still had a blaster in my hand and one strapped to my right thigh, although the one that I had strapped to my left thigh was gone. Must have dropped it when I tried to hurdle that damn thing.

A click-clack sound brought me back to reality. I snuck a peek through the rubble and saw two of the bugs heading my way. There would be no way for me to fight them, not with another ten a few meters behind.

I ducked back down, grabbed a piece of rubble from the ground, and threw it at a nearby building, breaking the window with a loud crash.

The Xathi changed their focus towards the building, stepping towards it.

It was a few dozen yards to the next street, but I was out of options. I ran.

As I turned the corner, I chanced a look back and saw the two Xathi chasing after me, their six legs propelling them faster than my injured two. I let out a string of curses as I pushed through the pain, trying to find a place to hide, or at least a place of advantage for my eventual confrontation with them.

I was maybe a hundred yards down the street when the click-clack of their feet became clearer. A quick look back confirmed my suspicions: they had rounded the corner, and, having seen me, began running faster.

I looked ahead of me and scanned the street as I ran. No handy debris to hide behind, no rubble, nothing useful.

Just a row of little shops. If I had been on furlough, this would have been a quaint little street to walk down...and waste my money on.

My mind logged them as I ran past, searching for anything that might help. A bakery, a small candy shoppe, clothing stores, a perfume shop, a jewelry store, and a quaint little cafe sitting next door to a small toy store. Each place looking very cute, organized, and clean, ready to open for business again the next day.

Now that the Xathi had arrived, they might never open again.

And throwing sandwiches at them wouldn't help at all.

The click-clacking got closer—so close, I didn't dare look back anymore. As I approached another corner, I *felt*, rather than heard, the Xathi attack.

I dove forward, tucking into a roll that brought me stumbling back to my feet. A quick glance as I rolled showed them only a few feet behind me, close enough to swing one of their "arms" at me. Had I not dived forward, the nail at the end of one of the claws would have cut the back of my shoulders, bringing me down.

Ignoring the pain as best as I could, I pushed harder

to reach the street corner. I wasn't sure if turning the corner would do me any good, but it was worth a shot.

I shot around the corner like a cannon blast and was relieved to find the street in shambles. So many places to hide.

I dove behind a turned-over delivery vehicle parked in front of a store with a picture of a hammer on the windows and sign advertising the place.

Wriggling, I tried to get as far under it as I could. The Xathi slowed down to a walk as they passed by me, their heads moved back and forth, searching.

I forced my breathing to slow, waiting for them to pass.

One.

Two.

They kept on, searching for me.

Quietly removing my other blaster from my hip, I limped behind them. In my peripheral vision, people watched, wide eyes focused on the Xathi.

Not a lot of difference in their shock when they saw me. Whatever.

They'd have to get over it.

Then one of the humans stumbled, the displaced rubble at his feet clattering into the street. The Xathi whirled, rearing up to strike with their whips.

In three quick leaps, I was behind the one on the left, firing.

It dropped to the ground, cracking and breaking before it hit the rubble.

The other bug spun towards me, the edge of its thick carapace cutting into my hand. With a grunt I pulled myself up and swung around.

There would be only one chance.

A bearded human ran into the street, shouting and waving his arms. Distracted, the Xathi froze.

Just the moment I needed.

With the two bugs dead, the rest of the humans came out of hiding, looking to the three men in the street.

Two of them waved for the refugees to follow them while the bearded one looked at me and stepped forward.

"Not friends of yours, then?" His voice was gruff, deep, and broken. I remembered that voice...it had been mine for the first year after the attack on Skota. He pointed at the two bugs as he spoke.

I shook my head. "No, enemies."

"Good. They're some mean bastards, but we got lucky." He turned away from me and brought up the rear of the ragtag group of survivors fleeing further into town.

"Lucky? How so?" I asked, and the man turned around.

"Thought it was all over when another group of

those things cornered us, but they toppled a tanning vat. Made them all jittery, and they began to walk funny. Oddly enough for us to slip away. Thought we were home free, until these two came at us."

He rejoined his group and they disappeared into the rubble.

What could have done that? I'd never heard of something disorienting the Xathi like that.

The smell?

Remembering the perfume store on the previous street, I started back towards it.

As I walked, I tried to reach out to Jeneva again.

I still couldn't find her. Either she was that good at blocking me, or she was dead.

There was no time for the stabbing in my chest. I'd mourn her like I mourned the rest of my family, one battle at a time.

The street was empty. A bit surprised at that, but it made sense. The Xathi were a hive mind, but the queens weren't stupid.

They weren't going to send any more soldiers out to find one enemy. Not when they were rounding up dozens of far easier prey. They had time on their side and the numbers to wait.

I spotted the perfume shop and tried the door, hoping against hope that it would open quietly.

It did—until a few inches in, when a damn bell

hanging above the door rang as the door hit it. I grabbed the bell, ripped it down, and stomped the damn thing into oblivion.

Ducking behind the perfume counter, I waited, looking out into the street, waiting for the Xathi to investigate the sound.

Nearly a hundred heartbeats passed before I was convinced nothing was coming. I searched the shop, testing different scents, trying to figure what would work together to create a strong enough smell to disorient those bastards.

While I did that, I kept trying to connect with Jeneva. I sought her out, tried every trick I knew to find her mental connection, but to no avail.

She was closed off to me. She was gone. The look on her face when she found out that we had brought the Xathi to her world...

It crushed me. It weakened me.

Why had I allowed myself to fall for this woman? Why had I allowed myself to *be* with this woman?

She wasn't Skotan. She wasn't one of the beauties of my home.

She wasn't any of those things.

She was simply Jeneva. And dead or alive, she was lost to me.

A horrible stench snapped me out of my misery.

In my angst and distraction, I had mixed several of

the perfumes together, creating an incredibly nauseating aroma. My stomach clenched at the strong, cloying scent trapped in the small space.

I took a deep breath and held it as I searched for a container to carry my new "weapon" in. Luckily, I found a mostly empty jug quickly and dumped the concoction in.

My first breath outside the shop was the most wonderful breath I had ever taken—for one whole second. Then the scent from the shop escaped and followed me.

It took until I arrived at the hardware store to finally escape the stench from the shop. Then I let a slow grin cover my face.

Inside a hardware store, unless humans were exceedingly stupid and idiotic, would be more things that I could use to create scent bombs to give myself a chance. Give the humans a chance. Unless the accident with the tanning vat had nothing to do with the smell, in which case we were all screwed.

Fantastic.

I spent the next half hour creating as many chemical scent bombs as I could carry, all the while still trying to connect to Jeneva.

I only stopped when I stepped out of the building.

No more time, no more energy.

I could focus on two emotions: reason and rage.

How do I kill the Xathi, and how many of the bastards can I take with me? That was all I needed to know.

I rounded the corner in time to see another group of humans being herded into a sled. As one of the humans fell, I realized it was a child holding a smaller, younger child.

One of the Xathi guards raised its whip, cracking the pavement next to the cowering child.

And that was it.

No more planning, no more strategy. No more control.

Kill them all.

I flung one of the dozens of thin glass balls filled with the noxious fluid at the carapace of the guard, not waiting to see if it had any effect before tagging its neighbor, and then the next.

Another squad turned towards me, only to receive another dose of the chemical bombs.

One by one they stiffened and staggered back, lurching for balance.

Except for the one by the children. It stumbled, spindly legs collapsing beneath it.

Falling towards the cowering children.

JENEVA

The plan was a long shot, but it was all we had.

Still in a daze, Shad modified a dozen howlers to work at the new frequency. The effect it had on the Xathi fragment was encouraging, but I doubted the results would be the same when we used the new howlers on the live ones.

The best I could hope for was a moderate interference in the hive mind.

I tried to recall everything Vrehx had told me about the Xathi.

My stomach clenched. I wished he was here now. I was still furious with him, but he was certainly useful. And that was all, I insisted to my traitorous thoughts.

"Now what?" Mac asked, panting.

We were on the roof of the building. It had taken

longer than I anticipated to navigate the precarious stairwells and corridors. Half of the roof behind us had completely caved in. I didn't know how much time we had before the rest of it gave out.

I surveyed the city below. Half of the Xathi corralled civilians onto shuttles to be loaded onto the Xathi ship that waited just outside Duvest's walls. The other half systematically checked the city for survivors, for anything they could use. Didn't know, didn't matter. They were down there, and deadly.

Blue soldiers moved in groups while black hunters silently stalked the streets alone.

I glared at the ship, its strange lines and geometries hurting my eyes, making no sense.

If this was just one of their attack ships, how much larger was the hive ship that had crashed?

My original plan had been to sneak onto the ship alone and plant the modified howlers.

But Tobias wouldn't allow it. "Renna would kill us both, even if we survived the Xathi. If we're going to do this, let's be smart."

"Are the howlers secured to the drones?" I asked. Shad and Tobias might be shady, and might be jerks - but Renna was right. They did tinker with all sorts of things.

Mac nodded.

"The Xathi we see are hunters and soldiers, but

there are queens and subqueens, as well. My guess? At last one is on the ship, overseeing everything."

Tobias tapped his fingers on the edge of the wall, staring at the ship. Probably wondering how to make a profit from it.

"We're going to send four drones down into the city. Concentrate on the largest groups of soldiers collecting slaves. If this works the way I hope it does, it will give the people in the city a chance to escape."

"And the rest?" Tobias asked.

"The rest go to the ship. It's my theory that if we disrupt the queens, the others will abandon the city to investigate," I concluded.

"*Theory?*" Mac started. "This is all just theoretical? Do you even know if these will have any effect on them at all?"

"Nope," I said honestly. "Got a better plan?"

"Cheery," Mac muttered, but he didn't argue further.

"Getting the drones to the Xathi on the ground will be easy," I said. "But the Xathi ship is massive. I have no idea what it looks like on the inside or where the queens are. We'll be going in almost completely blind."

The drone controllers were equipped with small screens so that we could get a live view of the area. However, the camera's field of vision was small, and there was no audio.

"We've got to do our best to keep the drones out of

the Xathi's reach," I continued. "As soon as one figures out that the drone is what's causing the disruption, they'll all know, and they'll try to attack. That will be difficult on the ship—but not impossible if we're smart and careful about this."

Everyone nodded.

"All right, gentlemen," I said, sucking in a deep breath and grabbing my controller.

In total, we were able to pilot eight of the drones at once, leaving four as backup. Tobias, Mac, Shad, and I were going to lead our drones to the ship while Mac's associates took care of the ground units.

I wasn't sure Shad should be piloting one of the drones in the first place, but he insisted. Besides, he seemed much more focused when he was working with his own tech.

The drones whirred to life and gracefully lifted off the roof. Four sped towards the Xathi ship, and the other four glided down into the city streets.

"If anyone sees a guy with red skin and a lot of guns, please let me know," I said.

"You hope that bastard is alive?" Tobias sputtered.

"Only so I can personally kick his alien ass when this is all over," I said dryly.

Lie. But now wasn't the time to detangle my feelings for him.

"Let me know when you four have your drones in

position," I instructed the ground team. I was anxious to see if the modified howlers would even work.

"I've got one hovering over a group of the fuckers now," one of Mac's men sneered. "It doesn't look like the howler's doing anything."

"Move it in closer," I ordered. I myself moved closer to him so I could look at the tiny screen built into the controller.

He was right; the Xathi didn't appear to be affected. Still, he lowered his drone in increments.

I was beginning to lose hope when one of the Xathi suddenly stopped. Its limbs twitched like it was trying to shake something off.

"A little lower," I urged.

The drone dropped a few more feet. The Xathi was *definitely* irritated now. Its movement was stuttering and uncoordinated.

Several other Xathi came to investigate and were caught up in the effect of the sonic frequency. In the far corner of the screen, I saw the people start to run.

We gave them a chance, I sighed inwardly.

"Approaching the ship," Shad called. I turned my attention back to my own drone.

"We've got to find a way in," I muttered.

Near the base of the ship, long ramps had been extended, leading up into the belly of the massive vessel. They looked like our best bet.

"Let's split up. We've got a lot of ground to cover."

We each took a different ramp. The inside was utilitarian, illuminated by harsh overhead lights. I switched my drone into terrestrial mode so it could scuttle along the walls near the ceiling.

"The ground team has those fuckers on the fritz," Mac said smugly. "Weird thing, though. There was a group of bugs already spazzed out before we got there."

"Huh," I answered, distracted by my screen. "Maybe those were just more sensitive or something. Keep hunting them." I turned corners at random, wandering aimlessly through the interior of the ship, my breathing tight. As far as I knew, unless we took out the subqueens, they'd just keep sending soldiers.

The corridors were small enough that whenever I did encounter a Xathi, they were instantly affected by the modified howler.

But we didn't know enough. Were they still coherent enough to send a warning to the rest of the hive?

"These things are coming out of the damn woodwork," Tobias grumbled.

"You must be getting close to something," I reasoned. I, too, was running into more and more Xathi.

The corridor my drone was in suddenly opened up into a cavernous chamber. I moved up as high as I could, keeping close to the wall. Angling the camera, I could see a cluster of Xathi that were almost translucent and bigger than the others.

"I think I found them," I exclaimed. "I'm going in. Keep me updated on what the Xathi on the ground do."

"You got it," one of Mac's men agreed.

I piloted my drone in the lair of the queens and lowered it slowly. At that angle, I couldn't see the queens on my screen.

"I see you!" Shad called to me. "I'm in the chamber. I think the queens are more resilient than the others."

"I'm not sure where I am," Tobias said. "There's a lot of controls. Maybe the ship's command center? If Xathi have engineers and navigators, messing them up might be a good idea."

"Anything that hurts them is a boon for us," I agreed. My drone suddenly dipped sideways. I could only assume one of the queen's legs clipped it.

"I can't get any closer without going down," I said. "Shad, get in here. Mac, where are you?"

"Fuck if I know," Mac snapped. "All these damn hallways look the same."

"I'm level with you now," Shad informed me.

"Hey, the Xathi in the city look like they're starting to frenzy," one of Mac's men called out. I took my eyes off my control to look down into the streets below. The Xathi were clawing at their heads, abandoning their whips, and scurrying back to their sleds.

"Shit, it's working!" I cried, feeling a surge of elation like I'd never felt in my life.

The Xathi made a messy retreat. Several sleds smashed into buildings, the sonic frequency blasting through the hive-mind from the subqueens affecting all of them.

"We fucking did it!" Tobias cheered. "They're so fucked up, they can't even fly right."

When the Xathi reached their ship, they were so disoriented, many smashed through their own hull. Black smoke poured from several gaping holes in the side of the ship.

"I think I found a navigator or something," Tobias chuckled grimly. "It's trying to activate something in the control room, but I'm totally screwing with him."

"Who said the end of the world couldn't be fun," I laughed with relief. Despite the horror, despite everything, we'd struck back.

The Xathi ship shifted awkwardly as it lifted off the ground.

Good.

I lowered my mental shields and let myself feel the relief from the people around me and the civilians below.

Then a deafening crack came from the Xathi ship and the madness and screams began again.

Shockwaves knocked me off my feet and the very earth beneath us trembled. I clung to the edge of the building as the remainder of the roof slowly disintegrated.

A crater smoldered in the city center.

Bastards.

They had fired one of their canons into the city even as they limped away. We might have pushed back, but they weren't going to leave us unpunished.

Still, they were leaving without their harvest of flesh.

I threw one elbow over the lip of the roof, then another, feet scrambling for purchase as I tried to take in the effects of their parting shot.

A flash of red.

My heart clenched.

A crowd ran from a building as it tottered and crumbled down.

And Vrehx dashed through the middle of them.

The wrong way, towards the collapsing building.

I threw down my mental shield, fighting through the overwhelming fear of the civilians, desperate to reach him with my mind.

Vrehx! I called out.

Why would he do that? It was suicide.

He stopped suddenly, scooping a human child into his arms. Above him, the building finally gave out, an avalanche of concrete and glass raining down on them. I screamed his name as I lost sight of him.

The building I clung to shuddered, an ominous groan rising from what was left of the walls.

"Kid, get out!" Tobias bellowed from a stubby ledge near the stairwell, where he and Mac held up a blinking Shad. A wide gap yawned between us. Too wide for me to jump, even on my best day.

And this certainly didn't qualify.

"Get down! Go on!" I shouted back, scouring the ledge for anything I could use.

I'd just found Vrehx again.

I wasn't about to lose him.

"You better make it out, kid," Tobias called over his shoulder as he half-carried Shad away. "I'm not explaining this to Renna."

There. A twisted length of pipe protruded from the building. Just a bit farther, and I could almost reach it.

My fingers slipped from the ledge, my arms flailing to catch the pipe.

With a gasp, I hit it and clutched it until my hands ached, panting for breath.

The pipe creaked, slowly bending under my weight. This was it. I couldn't run anymore.

Dust choked my lungs, and as the pipe angled down,

I could only cling tight, eyes closed, mind focused on one thought. *I'm sorry, Vrehx. Please be safe.*

Despite everything that had happened between us, I needed him.

Hell...maybe it was more than needed.

He *had* to be alive.

With a thud, the pipe struck the ground and my eyes flew open.

Street level. Or what was left of the street.

Mounds of rubble surrounded me, small fires flickered, survivors wandered, looking dazed.

And, at the center of it all, stood Vrehx, still holding the small child in his arms.

He stepped towards me, then stopped, uncertainty leaking through his barriers.

Words wouldn't suffice. Not for this.

I threw my mental door open, reaching for him, luxuriating in his warmth, his strength.

His heart.

"Jeneva," he said, coming closer to me.

We were in a war. Flames would consume our future. But right now, all I felt was relief.

And like the badass I was, I passed out.

"I don't understand why we can't just leave!" Leena stormed, pacing across one of the common spaces in the *Vengeance*.

"You'd really rather take your chances against the Xathi than stay here?" Axtin said in disbelief. "I doubt the Xathi would even take you as a slave. They'd probably kill you outright to preserve their sanity."

Leena looked like she was going to say more, but Mariella's soft voice silenced her.

"It's better to stay here, Leena."

Leena gave one curt nod before dropping the subject altogether. She didn't look happy at all.

"You," Axtin said, pointing to Mariella. "Teach me how to shut her up."

Mariella only smiled, the same sad smile she'd worn

since she'd left the med bay. Tu'ver, never far from her side, looked amused at Leena and Axtin's antics.

The normalcy was nice, but it was missing something.

Some*one*.

Vrehx had spent nearly all of his time in meetings with General Rouhr or in his cabin since our return from Duvest.

Cautiously, I reached out for him with my mind. From the feel of it, he was at his desk, pretending to look at paperwork.

I nodded goodbye to the others, but Amira approached me before I left.

"Hey," she said softly, her hands tucked away into her back pockets. She looked uneasy. "I'm glad you didn't die out there."

"Thanks," I smiled a little bit, unsure of how to begin. "I'm glad you're not a slave to a bunch of creepy crystal bugs."

"Yeah, me, too." She laughed once before a more serious expression took over her features. "Look, I'm sorry at how I've treated you since you technically rescued me. I'm still really pissed about how you took off to live in the middle of nowhere. I don't think I'm ready to forgive you for that. But…I'm willing to start working on it."

"I'm glad." I beamed.

Amira surprised me by hugging me. I gripped her tightly. Now that I knew how to control my empathic abilities, reconnecting seemed like a real possibility.

"I've got to get back to the refugee quarters," she said when she let go. "Now that we've got power, your aliens are fitting everyone they missed for those language transmitting devices. I'm going to make sure our people don't riot over it."

"I bet General Rouhr appreciates that," I said carefully. Amira helpful, not hating me, was different. Unsettling.

Several times, I almost talked myself out of my self-appointed mission. Once, I even made it halfway back to the common room before forcing myself to turn around.

When I knocked on his door, my hand shook.

I had almost run away again when the door slid open. Vrehx, blinking in surprised, gave me a small smile.

"I was beginning to think I'd never speak to you again," he said. He gestured for me to enter.

"I figured you'd be busy after Duvest," I said, mouth dry, taking care not to stand too close to him as I followed him into his quarters. My eyes fell on the bed, then bounced away, desperate to look anywhere else.

"I've been pretty busy," he admitted. "But I have been

wanting to talk to you. I thought I ought to give you space, though."

"That was probably a wise decision," I said with a nervous laugh.

I thought of Amira and how directly she said what she needed to say. No edging around it or sugarcoating. I needed to do that now.

I took a deep breath and faced Vrehx head on. "Vrehx, you betrayed my trust, and that's hard for me to deal with. I'm not used to trusting people, and I'm not good at it. I don't blame you for bringing the Xathi here. It's not your fault. I…I want to forgive you."

It all came out in a rush. By the time I was finished, my face was flushed, and my heart was pounding. I sounded like a complete dumbass.

"That's all a relief to hear," Vrehx said slowly, a smile spreading across his face. "And I want you to know that I'll do whatever it takes to win back your trust. You're important to me, Jeneva." His cheek darkened to a near-maroon. Was he flushing? "I … like you. Considerably."

He reached for my hand, and I laced my fingers with his, marveling again at our differences, how little they mattered after all was said and done.

He tilted his face to mine, a soft smile on his lips. "I give you permission to look into my mind and see for yourself exactly how much." His eyes glimmered with mischief and I found myself laughing.

"I 'like' you, too, Vrehx," I said, wondering exactly how much 'liking' he was talking about.

Or I was.

In an instant, his arms encircled me, every hard curve of muscle pressed up against me.

When he used two fingers to tip my chin up, I didn't object. He lowered his head and pressed his lips to mine, kissing me deeply. I wound my arms around his neck, pulling him closer, drinking in his taste until I was dizzy from the intensity of him. Of us.

He pulled away far too soon, leaving me breathless.

"What should we do now?" he asked with a wicked smile.

I trailed my fingers up his arms, delighting in his small shivers. This man. This strange, powerful man.

And he was mine.

"We have a lot of work ahead of us," I said, leading him as I walked backwards towards the bed. "But, right now, I think you deserve a night off."

"I couldn't agree more," he replied. "But what do you think I should do with that night?"

He looked at me, waiting for my answer.

And it was a very human one.

One word to let him know all was well with us.

"Me."

OH MY GOODNESS!

I've had the Conquered World in my head for so long, and I'm thrilled to get to finally share it with you!

I hope you enjoyed spending time with Jeneva and Vrehx. Next up, Axtin and a certain feisty chemist - and the sparks are going to fly!

Keep reading for a sneak peek or just grab your copy now!

RATHER DIVE **into the Conquered World for an extended stay? The boxset of the first 10 books is available now!**

XOXO,

Elin

AXTIN: SNEAK PEAK

L eena

"You can't be serious!"

I clenched and unclenched my hands to stop them from shaking. It was all I could do to keep my voice even. I could feel my nails digging into my palm.

"Try to think about it logically, Leena," Mariella suggested. Her usually musical voice was grating. My temper flared and snapped, but I reeled it in.

"I'm the only one on this entire fucking ship capable of thinking *logically*," I spat. "You're insane for thinking you're safer on this ticking time bomb of a ship."

Why couldn't she understand? Technically, now that the *Vengeance* had a sustainable power source and the cloaking device was working, the Xathi couldn't see it. Nevertheless, I wouldn't call that safe because we still knew next to nothing about the aliens we'd been living alongside.

"I'm alive because Tu'ver brought me here," Mariella said. I scoffed.

"Who knows why he really brought you here? He could have intended to use you as a hostage…or a concubine," I sneered. I had to believe that Mariella was being willfully ignorant of the danger she was putting herself in, and me by extension.

"That's an ugly thing to say," she remarked with a bite in her mild voice.

She turned away from me to look at a false window with a holographic projection of a garden. Her dark wavy hair fell across her cheek.

"The longer we spend on this ship, the less time we have to find a cure," I said.

Mariella didn't look at me. She didn't speak. I stood for a moment, and let the familiar feeling of helplessness wash over me.

I rejected it, shoving it deep down inside me. If she wanted to act like a child, fine. I had other things to do, anyway.

I left the room without saying another word.

Earlier that morning, I'd been told that the captain

of the *Vengeance,* General Rouhr, wanted to meet with me. I couldn't imagine why.

I didn't think he knew who I was. I certainly didn't know who he was. I'd kept my contact with the aliens at a minimum since I arrived on this ship, unlike Mariella and the other woman, Jeneva.

Mariella preferred to spend her time looking at imaginary gardens and talking to Tu'ver. Jeneva was actually *with* one of the red ones now. If they wanted to risk their lives like that, who was I to stop them?

Sure as hell didn't mean I trusted any of them.

I strode through the sliding metal doors of one of the com rooms. General Rouhr, a rugged-looking Skotan with a scar running down the left side of his face, greeted me with a nod. My gaze flickered to the others in the room.

I was surprised to see Jeneva there. She smiled at me. I didn't smile back.

When I first met her, she was prickly and unfriendly. I didn't fully understand what had changed about her.

The Skotan she'd become enamored with sat next to her. I believed his name was Vrehx. He was the only one on the ship I didn't mind, and he had the good sense not to bother me.

My gaze settled on the hulking form of a green

Valorni. Jagged purple bands stretched over his broad shoulders and along his thick arms.

Oh, hell.

This *creature* was a living, breathing personification of a migraine. Axtin was brash, thickheaded, and impulsive—everything I hated. What the hell could he possibly be doing here?

"Ms. Dewitt, thank you for coming," General Rouhr said.

It was strange hearing him speak in my language. The ear transmitter, one of the things they'd given us when we'd first arrived, had somehow taught the aliens our language.

Once I learned I could understand them without the transmitter, I insisted they remove it. I didn't like the idea of alien tech crawling around in my brain—and it literally did crawl. I'd never forget the horrible way it felt when it was first inserted into my ear canal.

Mariella and Jeneva had elected to leave theirs in. Because of this, they knew considerably more of the alien's tongue than I did. I'd also made a point to avoid as much contact as possible, so there's that.

"Will this take long?" I asked tightly.

"Why? You've got somewhere else to be?" Axtin smirked. I didn't even dignify his response with a glare.

"I'll be as brief as possible," the general said with an

understanding nod. "We've received a message from Duvest, the last city that was hit by the Xathi."

I remembered. It was a devastating attack. Duvest was the manufacturing capital of the planet, and many labs relied on the equipment produced there.

"It seems," he continued, "that there is a group of people working to develop a weapon against the Xathi —some kind of a scent bomb, as I understand it. However, they have run into some problems developing the formula. I've recommended you to them."

"Why?" I demanded. I hadn't told anyone about my work or my research. I clenched my jaw and squeezed my hands into fists, shoving my temper down.

"Mariella mentioned you studied chemistry," Vrehx offered. I cursed, low enough that only myself could hear it. Mariella had no right to talk about my life to them.

But despite my anger, the idea of working again sent a jolt of excitement down my spine. I missed being in a lab. I felt more at home there than anywhere else.

Regardless of my distrust of the aliens around me, I did want this war to end. I wanted the Xathi gone.

"Do you have more information?" I asked General Rouhr.

He slid a thin data pad across the table to me. Displayed on the screen was a detailed plan for the bomb and several potential chemical formulas. I could already see a few places where the formulas could be improved.

I wondered what their lab setup was like. The city was hit pretty hard. I doubted they had as much as they needed.

What supplies were available to them? Who was working on this? How did they know for sure that the Xathi are sensitive to smells?

"I can see the crazy wheels turning in her head," Axtin muttered.

I resisted the urge to throw the data pad at him. He was right, anyway. My mind was whirling, and it felt amazing.

Another thought struck me...

If the people in Duvest were able to send these notes, then they had network access. There was a chance, albeit a small one, that I could recover my own research notes from their lab. And if their lab was as good as I hoped it was, I could remain in Duvest to work on finding a cure.

"I'd be happy to help." I smiled at General Rouhr. He blinked once, the only indication that he was surprised by my quick response.

"Excellent," he responded. "I'll send a message back telling them to expect you. Jeneva?"

Jeneva pulled out a map of the region and laid it flat on the table.

"I took the liberty of marking out the quickest and safest way to get there," she explained. She swiped a hand over the map, and a three-dimensional holograph grid rose up between us. A glowing blue line snaked across the map, marking my theoretical path.

"This way avoids any known animal breeding grounds, environmental instabilities, and other hazards," Jeneva continued.

Though I didn't know much about her, I knew she lived in the wilds of the forest alone for an impossibly long time. I had enough good sense to take her word for it when it came to matters of survival.

"That doesn't look too bad," I ventured.

Duvest wasn't as far away as I'd thought it was. If I stuck with Jeneva's path, I'd be fine.

Besides, I wasn't completely helpless out in the forest. I'd managed to track down Mariella in the dingy backwater she'd been living in.

Before I could stop myself, I imagined what it might have been like if I hadn't decided to find her.

Would the aliens have found her? Would she even be alive now? Would *I* even be alive now?

I forced my mind to go quiet. Making room for those thoughts wouldn't do me any favors.

Mariella was alive. I was alive. That's all that mattered.

"I think it'll take the two of you a little more than a

day to get to Duvest," Jeneva went on, completely unaware of how quickly my heart was beating.

"Two?" I asked, almost missing what Jeneva said.

"You didn't think we were going to send you out there alone, did you?" Vrehx chimed in, his brow furrowed in what might have been true concern...or maybe he just thought I was stupid. It was hard to tell with him.

"She wouldn't last an hour out there alone," Axtin scoffed, folding his arms across his broad chest.

I wasn't keen on making that trek alone, but now I wanted to show that arrogant prick I could.

"You're right," General Rouhr agreed. I bristled before I noticed something like amusement gleaming in his eyes. "That's why you'll be going with her."

"What?" Axtin and I blurted at the same time.

"He'll get us killed before the *Vengeance* is even out of sight!" I exclaimed.

That moron sought out a fight whenever he got the chance. He'd lead me right into a den of some awful, poison-spitting monster just for the fun of it.

"I want both of you ready to depart within the hour," General Rouhr commanded, completely ignoring our protests. "Dismissed."

AXTIN

Great. I have to play babysitter. So be it.

My thoughts about this whole thing ranged from joy at being able to do something again and pure hatred at the idea that I was playing bodyguard to this...female.

Srell.

I took the slow way down to the armory, not wanting to give her the satisfaction of thinking that I rushed on her account. I punched in my code and took in a deep breath of that beautiful aroma.

How I wish they'd just let me sleep in here. Why won't they allow me to keep more than a blaster in my personal quarters? I mean, I understand the need to keep an accurate inventory and all, but dammit, why can't I keep my toys with me? Huh? What's so bad about that?

I looked around at what was easily my second favorite room, right behind the training facility.

To my left were the blasters, rifles, Tu'ver's personal sniper rifles, our ever-dwindling stash of grenades and smoke bombs, and some hand-to-hand weapons. The wall in front of me was where the packs and survival gear were kept.

I went there first, ignoring my little corner to the right. I grabbed two packs and loaded them with rations, ammunition, sleep packs, and med kits.

Thinking about how small Leena was, I took more of the ammo and rations, giving myself the heavier pack.

Making sure I didn't forget anything, I turned to my corner.

Oh, the memories and toys!

I'm not like Tu'ver. I don't have built-in augmentations like his people do. But I did like the idea of being augmented when necessary.

Wonder if I need any of them now...

I spent a few minutes trying to decide if I needed my augments or not, then decided to just grab weapons and go. I grabbed my three blasters, strapping one to my left hip, one to my right hip, and the other behind my back. Then I grabbed my rifle, double-checking it and leaning it against the packs, and then I reached for my pride and joy.

She was a work of art, handmade over hundreds of hours, thousands of tiny changes to make her *just* right, and dozens upon dozens of designs and alloy combinations to get the weight exactly the way it was.

I loved my hammer. It was massive, even I needed both hands to wield her. She had cost me a fortune just finding the right metals that were both lightweight and super strong.

Her handle was wrapped in a combination of Tyit leather and a Skotan fabric, giving me a super tight grip no matter how sweaty or bloody my hands get. She was the perfect close-range weapon against the Xathi. I could crack one of those bastards open with a single swing.

I put on the special harness I had made for her, then strapped her to my back.

I need to name you one of these days, I thought as I grabbed a sonic-net and a thigh-pack of grenades.

I made sure to double-check everything again just to make sure before I headed down to the cargo bay we were using to leave the ship.

There she was, waiting impatiently for me. When she saw me, she gave me this *hurry up* look, then stomped over towards the bay door, ignoring her sister as she passed by her.

Hmm, not that I care, but I wonder why she's ignoring her now after she was so insistent on staying with her before.

I caught up to her, handing her pack to her as I walked by to open the door.

We walked out, the door closed behind us, and we headed out. It was excruciating walking in silence—I couldn't stand it.

"Why didn't you say goodbye to your sister?" I asked, trying to break the ice.

Oh, the look she flashed me. If we could *weaponize* that look, the war with the Xathi would be over faster than we could process the idea.

"What does it matter to you?" she answered, obviously annoyed.

I could surmise that I had angered the female. "Honestly? It doesn't. I was just trying to make small talk."

"Well, you failed…miserably." *You think?* "Not that it's any of your business, but there's no point in saying goodbye to someone you're going to see again anyway."

"Okay," I said, putting my hands up to show that I was harmless. She stormed on ahead, leaving me to catch up. As I caught up to her, she looked me up and down, making me wonder if she was sizing me up for approval or not.

"So, why aren't you wearing that…that…disguise thing that you people have?"

"I don't need it."

"What the hell do you mean that you *don't need it*?"

I flashed her my sweetest smile and tried to put on a nonchalant face. "The whole planet is covered in different life forms, and your kind need to get used to the idea. That's why I don't need it. Besides, the people of…"

I tried to remember the name of the city we were going to. I was a little embarrassed by the fact that I couldn't remember the place. I was never good with names.

"Duvest," she said in a very mocking tone.

"Yeah. The people of Duvest already know about us anyway, so there's even less need to use it there."

I watched as she thought about this, then she shrugged and turned her back to me and started walking.

Hmm, not bad.

I shook my head, bit back a smile, and followed after her. We had barely been walking twenty minutes when she became a major pain in my rumpus.

She was stomping around, or at least it looked like she was stomping. She didn't bother being cautious of where she was walking, seemingly snapping every single twig, branch, and stick that was on the entire forest trail.

I was cringing at every snap, every crack, and every curse coming from ahead of me. Enough was enough. I had to say something.

"Excuse me… Um…excuse me? Miss no-sense-of-danger-or-understanding-the-need-for-quiet? Can we *not* step on every single branch in the forest or make an unreasonable amount of noise? Everything on your planet wants to kill everything else, and now the Xathi are here as well. So if you don't mind, I'd really like to not have to fight *everything* there is at every step."

I should have realized the mistake I made as soon as I started speaking, but I didn't.

"Excuse the shit out of me?" Her voice started to get

a little higher with each word. "You've been on this rock only a short time, whereas I've been here my whole damn life. Don't you dare presume to tell me when I should and shouldn't be careful. Right now, we're nowhere near the *dangerous* parts of the forest. And as for your damn Xathi, that's what you're here for, isn't it?"

Srell, this woman was an aggravation, but she had a spirit that fit my people. She would have been a fine Valorni.

"Well? Isn't that why you're here? To *be* my bodyguard and fight off the monsters?" she asked.

"Yes. Yes, I am. Now, as your bodyguard, I suggest walking a bit quieter, a bit nicer, and maybe keeping an eye out around you for anything. With us and the Xathi here, this might not be a safe part of the forest anymore," I retorted.

"Fine."

She walked away from me again, but at least she was quiet about it this time. We walked for nearly an hour in silence before I made another mistake.

"I have an honest question for you," I asked.

With a normal voice that took me by surprise—I hadn't heard it from her before—she responded with a simple, "What's that?"

"All you have to do is double-check an equation for a formula, yes?" I confirmed.

"Yeah," she answered.

"Couldn't we have done that from the *Vengeance*? Why did we have to risk danger to travel there?" I followed up.

She stopped dead in her tracks, forcing me to stop and look back at her. The look on her face made me realize, finally, that I had made that mistake.

"Really?" she asked, clearly exasperated this time. "You think my job is *so* easy that I can just do everything remotely? That I don't need to be hands-on? That I can do it while sitting on the toilet? Is that what you think?"

"Well, no…I just…" I never got to say another word.

She went into an absolute tirade, ripping into me about my lack of intelligence, how I was just a jock—whatever that was—and how this was her life, her passion, and that she can't just *do* it from some room on a *god-forsaken alien trash can*.

She kept going for what seemed like forever before I heard something. I tried to quiet her, but she just took it as another dig at who she was and what she did and proceeded to get louder. I still heard the sound through the slight pauses in her verbal attack.

Something was coming.

Then they crashed out of the trees nearby, five of those Luurizi things—enough to be a herd. They were little *delicate* creatures, with poisonous barbs on their hooves. They jumped high in the air, their hooves aimed right at Leena's head.

They never made it there.

I caught one of the creatures, bounced it off the ground, and snapped its neck, turning its head clean around a full rotation.

Then I took my blaster and shot three of them in quick succession, knocking them back, rendering them immobile.

The remaining one changed its trajectory and then ran away as it saw its herd decimated.

"Oh my God. Oh my God." Leena kept repeating over and over, staring at the creature as it twitched on the ground.

I grabbed her and pulled her close, wrapping her in my arms. "I have you. I'll keep you safe."

Why am I letting myself feel for her like this? Why do I care about her own blasted feelings right now? She's annoying, she's stubborn, she's stupid—not really, she's brilliant, and she knows things I'd never hope to understand, but she's stupid on basic things—and she drives me crazy.

Then I noticed her eyes on me, her quickened breathing, and the look behind the shield she had put up. There was something there that I'd never noticed before. I chuckled to myself.

She was barely tall enough to reach my chest. Her blonde hair was in stark contrast to my brown, and her slim figure was dwarfed by my hulk. Something inside me screamed out to take her, to take her right now and make her mine.

Srell.

I knew right from that moment that there was something special about this female. But we had a job to do, and if we didn't get it done soon, there wouldn't be a chance for me to find out what. I pulled away from her.

I cleared my throat to get my voice back. "We should get going, before anything else shows up." I started walking.

LEENA

My hands shook, my breath coming in uneven gasps as I followed Axtin further down the path.

I told myself that it was the Luurizi attack, that I was just shaken from the near-death experience, but the lie felt hollow even in my own mind.

Sure, almost being impaled by a wild animal was unsettling—there was no denying that. But it was what I felt in Axtin's arms that had truly shaken me. Even then, walking several feet behind him, I could still feel him, the press of him against me, the heat of his emerald skin.

I groaned, shoving the thoughts from my mind with

force.

Obviously, I reasoned with myself, the past few days had affected me even more than I had realized. The trauma of everything had finally been catching up to me—sure, that was it.

Because clearly, I wasn't actually attracted to Axtin. For fuck's sake, he wasn't even a human being.

Feeling reassured of my relative sanity, I hurried my steps, closing the distance between us.

It wasn't exactly the simplest task. Axtin was, after all, a great deal larger than me. His long legs ate up the distance ahead of us, and I rushed to catch up to him.

I ignored the way my hands picked right up shaking as I got near him, just as I ignored the sound of my own pounding heart.

I had more important things to focus on after all, like save the world.

"Are you okay?" he asked, his voice quiet, gruff.

"Fine."

He turned his head slightly, eyeing me slowly. For a moment, I thought he'd speak, but he clearly thought better of it, turning his attention back towards the path.

I watched him from the corner of my eye, feeling unable to control my gaze. The sunlight played wonders on his skin, reflecting brilliantly off the deep green, off the bands of purple that stood in stark contrast to the rest of him.

He seemed to walk with extra care since the attack, his eyes constantly roving over our surroundings. Every now and then, he'd quicken his pace, hurrying ahead to move a fallen log from the path or peek around a blind. His attention felt odd, personal somehow, and I found it almost impossible to look away.

It wasn't until his eyes met mine again that I even realized how long I'd been staring. Quickly, feeling like a child, I bowed my head, staring in rapt fascination at the thick carpeting of leaves beneath my feet.

I tried my best to focus on the real issue at hand, redirecting my thoughts back to the scent bombs. I had a fairly good memory of the formulas I'd already seen. If I could just focus on it, I might come up with a good solution before we even arrived in Duvest.

Try as I might, though, my thoughts seemed beyond my control. One moment, I'd be reciting a formula in my mind; the next, I'd find myself once again staring at Axtin's hulking form.

I groaned inwardly, frustrated at my own behavior for once.

What on earth was wrong with me?

We walked in silence for a long while, my thoughts twirling strangely through my mind. I don't know how long we went on like that. It seemed like hours, though I knew it was far less.

Axtin was the first to break the silence, slowing his gait to turn towards me.

"Are you sure you're okay?"

"I'm fine, Axtin. Why?"

"I just—" He seemed to stumble over his words, unsure how to continue.

"What?"

"I didn't do anything, did I? Like hurt or scare you, I mean."

I scoffed in amusement, completely caught off guard by the question.

"No, trust me. You couldn't, even if you wanted to."

He tilted his head, his features contorting into an expression I'd never seen on him before. He looked surprised, hurt even.

But more surprising than his reaction was my own. To my utter amazement, I immediately regretted my words. Sure, Axtin got under my skin from time to time —or most of the time. But it had never been my intention to hurt him.

I opened my mouth to tell him as much, but found myself at a loss for words. I had never encountered anyone who could make me trip over my own thoughts like this before. It was utterly infuriating.

I reached up, running my fingers through my hair in irritation as I struggled to come up with a coherent thought.

I was just opening my mouth to try again when the sound reached my ears.

My teeth slammed shut with an audible click, my head whipping around wildly in search of the source.

"Leena." I heard Axtin say, but my attention was elsewhere.

Somewhere, near from the sound of it, someone was crying—a child.

I spun in a circle, searching the trees as my heart started to thump wildly in my chest.

What would a child be doing all the way out here?

Had the Xathi found them?

After a moment that felt like an eternity, I stilled, focusing on the direction I was now sure the sound was coming from.

"It's coming from over there," I said, pointing towards a dense thicket.

"Leena, it's not—"

I didn't wait to hear what he had to say—I couldn't. With every passing second, my fear only seemed to grow. I knew something was wrong, and I couldn't simply stand around and talk it out with Axtin.

I surged forward before I'd even fully decided to, my feet kicking up clouds of dirt as I propelled myself into the thickening forest. With every step, the sound seemed to grow louder, beckoning me on like a siren.

My mind spun through a million possibilities for

what might lay ahead, each grimmer than the last. I clenched my fists, struggling to find a sense of control in the sudden chaos.

I could hear Axtin calling my name from somewhere back in the trees, his voice laced with near panic. I understood his worry, feeling a deep sense of dread pool in my own chest, as well.

Still, I raced onward, unwilling to let my growing fear stop me. Somewhere in these trees was a child in need of help. I could never look at myself the same way again if I didn't do anything to help the poor thing.

The trees thinned around me, space opening up in the dense foliage. The cries grew even nearer, seeming impossibly close.

Finally, panting, I broke into a small clearing. My body quivered from the exertion, sweat beading my forehead as I looked wildly about for the source of the cries.

I was so panicked, I nearly missed her. She sat in the shade of a nearby tree, her dark hair was matted, falling around her in waves as she buried her face in her hands. The cries only seemed to grow louder as I approached, one hand extended before me in what I hoped would be seen as a sign of peace.

"Hello? Don't be afraid. I want to help," I said.

She didn't move, didn't say a word. Her cries

continued unabated, her small shoulders shaking in the intensity of her pain.

"Are you hurt?" I asked softly, still inching my way towards her.

Still nothing. It was like she didn't even know I was there.

"Everything's going to be okay. I'm going to help you." I was nearly whispering, trying my best not to frighten her as I finally closed the distance between us.

I should have known that something was wrong— the way she ignored me, the way she seemed utterly oblivious to my presence. It should have been obvious that things weren't what they seemed.

My own fear made me completely unaware, though.

"Sweetie?" I asked, reaching down to touch her.

I expected her to jump, maybe even to scream at my touch, but she didn't—though I suppose that makes sense, given that I never touched her at all.

My hand passed neatly through her, disappearing into the pale white of her shoulder. I felt nothing—no resistance, nothing.

My thoughts seemed to stutter, logic failing me in my shock.

I reached for her again, only to watch my hand pass once more through the shaking child at my feet.

I looked around dazedly, feeling my eyes widen in fear.

And that's when the walls went up around me.

The forest floor sprang to life, beams of energy seeming to jump from the earth itself. I was instantly encased, trapped on all sides by the neatly spaced beams that created a wall around the air.

Time seemed to slow as my mind spun painfully, desperately trying to make sense of this newest twist. In utter horror, I took in the cage that now surrounded me, my gaze whipping from it to the still sobbing child now safely outside of its walls.

My thoughts seemed to slow even as my heart began to race.

That's when I started to scream.

PLEASE DON'T FORGET TO LEAVE A REVIEW!

Readers rely on your opinions, and your review can help others decide on what books they read. Make sure your opinion is heard and leave a review where you purchased this book! books2read.com/u/4Ex2PO

For a free short story, opportunities for advance review copies, release news and the occasional cat picture, please join the newsletter!
https://elinwynbooks.com/newsletter-signup/

And don't forget the Facebook group, where I post sneak peeks of chapters and covers!
https://www.facebook.com/groups/ElinWyn/

DON'T MISS THE STAR BREED!

Given: Star Breed Book One

When a renegade thief and a genetically enhanced mercenary collide, space gets a whole lot hotter!

Thief Kara Shimsi has learned three lessons well - keep her head down, her fingers light, and her tithes to the syndicate paid on time.

But now a failed heist has earned her a death sentence - a one-way ticket to the toxic Waste outside the dome. Her only chance is a deal with the syndicate's most ruthless enforcer, a wolfish mountain of genetically-modified muscle named Davien.

The thought makes her body tingle with dread-or is it heat?

Mercenary Davien has one focus: do whatever is necessary to get the credits to get off this backwater mining colony and back into space. The last thing he wants is a smart-mouthed thief - even if she does have the clue he needs to hunt down whoever attacked the floating lab he and his created brothers called home.

Caring is a liability. Desire is a commodity. And love could get you killed.

https://elinwynbooks.com/star-breed/

ABOUT THE AUTHOR

I love old movies – *To Catch a Thief, Notorious, All About Eve* — and anything with Katherine Hepburn in it. Clever, elegant people doing clever, elegant things.

I'm a hopeless romantic.

And I love science fiction and the promise of space.

So it makes perfect sense to me to try to merge all of those loves into a new science fiction world, where dashing heroes and lovely ladies have adventures, get into trouble, and find their true love in the stars!

Printed by Amazon Italia Logistica S.r.l.
Torrazza Piemonte (TO), Italy

16747592R00183